Deceptions
Can Be
Murder

Connie Shelton

Deceptions
Can Be
Murder

Charlie Parker Mysteries, Book 23

Connie Shelton

Secret Staircase Books

Deceptions Can Be Murder
Published by Secret Staircase Books, an imprint of
Columbine Publishing Group, LLC
PO Box 416, Angel Fire, NM 87710

Book layout and design by Secret Staircase Books
Cover images © Jana Jurkova, Artspace, Lom6605, Majivecka
First trade paperback edition: January, 2025
First e-book edition: January, 2025

* * *

Publisher's Cataloging-in-Publication Data

Shelton, Connie
Deceptions Can Be Murder / by Connie Shelton.
p. cm.
ISBN 978-1649142016 (paperback)
ISBN 978-1649142023 (e-book)

1. Charlie Parker (Fictitious character)—Fiction. 2. New
Mexico—Fiction. 3. Private Investigators—Fiction. 4. Women
sleuths—Fiction. I. Title

Charlie Parker Mystery Series : Book 23.
Shelton, Connie, Charlie Parker mysteries.

BISAC : FICTION / Mystery & Detective.

813/.54

For Dan and Daisy, my pack, always.

Prologue

The van appeared on a Tuesday. Violet Merkle noted it on her calendar because she noted *everything* on her calendar. There wasn't a lot new and different in this little town at this time of year. The weather was hot, the cicadas seemingly the only creatures who loved it, and few people drifted out to her remote neighborhood. She'd followed her normal morning routine—dusting the living room furniture, vacuuming throughout the double-wide, taking pride in her immaculate housekeeping skills.

By noon, she had fixed her usual turkey and cheese sandwich and sat down to watch her shows. It was the rattling sound of an older vehicle that caught her attention. She had only three neighbors and knew the sounds of each of their vehicles intimately. Violet always congratulated herself on her observational expertise and knowing what was going on in the tiny development that never quite took off as it was supposed to in the 1970s.

When the noisy vehicle didn't drive on past, she set her sandwich aside and stood up, peering through the sheer lace curtains that faced the road. The panel van chugged to a stop in the vacant field across and slightly to the east of Violet's place. With a huff of dark exhaust, it quit.

She took in the details with a practiced eye: yellow paint job (not in great shape), some kind of a business logo that was faded and peeling, a dented front fender, Texas plates, a young couple in the front seats. The girl was driving (hard to get details because of the midday glare on the windshield). He had a tattooed arm resting on the passenger side window edge. The van hadn't been washed in ages, as evidenced by mud spatters along the sides and a heavy coating of dust all over.

Conclusions: These kids were dirt poor. And they weren't familiar with the area. They could have coasted another mile, where Old Route 66 headed downhill, and they would have landed right at Elroy's Garage. They'd be a lot better off with him than stuck out here in an empty field where there was only one old lady to ask for help.

Would they come up to her door and ask to use the phone? She hoped not. She didn't want to be uncharitable, but it wasn't smart for a lone woman to open the door to strangers, especially not a pair as scruffy as these.

She watched as both doors opened and the young couple got out. They were barely out of their teens, she guessed. The girl had extra-short hair that lay flat against her head in the heat. It was a shade of burgundy that came from Clairol, not Mother Nature. The kid—and she had to think of him as a kid, he had that immature look—was tall and lean with dark hair that fell over his forehead. Both arms were tattooed clear to the edges of his t-shirt. Not that Violet held judgement against tattoos, per se. But is that what you want to spend your money on when you can't even afford a car that runs?

She checked herself. You don't know their story, she reminded.

A shout went up behind her. Someone had won a jackpot on *The Price is Right*, and she'd missed it. And Muffin, her yellow tabby, was nibbling at the edge of Violet's sandwich. She turned from the window and shouted, "Scat!"

Chapter 1

Imentally went through the contents of my closet as I pulled away from the gray and white Victorian, leaving the office for the day. Tonight was Drake's big event and I was expected to dress up, not something that's usually on my Top Ten list, at all.

Victoria, my sister-in-law, had offered me a simple black dress and even I had to admit it was classic and cute, and it fit me like a glove. It was most likely the one I would end up wearing. My dressy holiday outfit was full-length, and that seemed a bit much for what was, in reality, a roomful of helicopter pilots and business owners.

Drake's pickup truck was already home, and I spotted Gram and Dottie getting out of Dottie's sedan next door as I pulled into my own driveway. Freckles bounded out of the back seat of my Jeep and headed toward Dottie, who always seemed to have a biscuit in one of her pockets.

"You're spoiling this dog," I called out, trotting slightly to keep up with the little beggar.

"Oh, Freckle-baby ain't spoiled, is she?" Dottie handed over a treat and was already reaching for a second one.

"Believe me, she is." I laughed and hitched my tote bag strap up higher on my shoulder.

Elsa, my surrogate grandmother, walked around the car and reached out to give me a hug. I noticed her fluffy white head barely came up to my shoulder anymore.

"We're going to have a bumper crop of apricots this year," she said. "Be ready."

A lot of years ago, she and I would get together as each of her fruit crops became ripe. We'd spend days making jam, putting the harvest up in jars, and freezing some. But my life seems to have become crazy-busy in recent times and it's just easier to buy what Drake and I need for household use. Still, I try to lend a hand so Dottie, as caregiver, doesn't have a ton of household work to do. We invite people in the neighborhood to help with the picking, and most of the produce itself goes to the local churches and food banks.

I gave Gram a hug and then reached down to clip a leash on Freckles. "Just give me a call when you need me."

"Should be within a couple of weeks for the apricots and cherries," Elsa said, facing Dottie for confirmation. "But we'll have snap beans and cucumbers ready to pick soon."

"Tonight be your big shindig, huh, Charlie?" Dottie had persuaded Freckles to sit still by holding yet another treat within sight.

"It is. Drake is getting a pretty important safety award.

Fifteen thousand flight hours without an accident or incident."

Both of the older ladies nodded with somewhat blank looks.

"It means a lot more to pilots than anyone else. But that's what this whole event is, a bunch of pilots gathering all in one place."

"We'll let you know about the apricots," Elsa called out, as I got my dog under control and headed home, while they walked toward her front door.

I found my husband in the bedroom wearing boxers and a white shirt.

"Will you be ready to leave in thirty minutes?"

"Depends. Do you think I need a shower? I had one this morning." I raised my hair off my neck and let him take a sniff. The sniff turned into a throaty growl and hands found their way under my shirt. "Okay, you start that and neither of us will be ready in a half hour."

He laughed and backed away. "You're fine, as long as you don't spend ages on your hair and makeup and that kind of girly stuff."

I shot him a look. Hair and makeup and girly stuff are definitely not my forte. In less time than it took him to step into trousers and do up his tie, I'd shed my office attire and slipped into the black dress and heels. I gathered my hair into a messy bun and applied a smear of lip gloss. By the time he had his dinner jacket on, I was standing at the door.

He went into the kitchen and scooped kibble into the dog's bowl, locked the back door, and we were headed downtown.

* * *

The chandeliers of the Grand Albuquerque Hotel ballroom cast a golden glow over the crowd of Albuquerque's elite. This was the venue for the awards ceremony, the culmination of the weeklong helicopter convention, which had somehow landed at the Albuquerque Convention Center this year. Drake and I had attended these events in Dallas and once in Las Vegas, but this was the first time our city played host.

I smoothed down my borrowed black cocktail dress and looked at the glittering crowd, feeling like a duck in a swan pond. Give me jeans and a faded tee any day over this getup.

"Champagne, ma'am?" A waiter appeared at my elbow, proffering a tray of bubbling flutes.

I accepted one, mainly to give my hands something to do as I scanned the room. I recognized several pilots and helicopter operators I'd met through Drake over the years. Then there was the usual assortment of politicians and local TV personalities, not to mention bigwigs from Bell Helicopter, Eurocopter, and Augusta—all here for the aviation gala of the year.

A warm hand settled on the small of my back. "Did I happen to mention … you look beautiful, my darling," Drake murmured, his breath tickling my ear.

I turned, taking in the sight of my husband in his tailored suit. Even after years of marriage, the sight of Drake Langston still made my heart skip a beat. "You clean up pretty good yourself, flyboy."

Some people thought we made an odd pair—me, an accountant and part owner of a private investigation firm, and Drake, the dashing helicopter pilot. But our shared love of adventure and knack for finding trouble made us a perfect match. He'd even taught me to fly his helicopter and I'd gone along on quite a few of his jobs.

I squared my shoulders. "Are you ready for your award?"

"A little nervous, I'll admit." He tugged at his tie once more. "I didn't really come up with any kind of speech. Do you think I need to?"

"It's these guys who should be talking about you and your achievements. Your record is impressive. I'm pretty sure you can just get by with saying thank you."

"Good. That's about all they'll get."

We wove through the crowd, Drake charming and comfortable in this crowd, while I oscillated between awkward smiles and rambling small talk. These folks knew Drake from his years crisscrossing the country, but I felt a bit out of my depth when the conversation turned to tail rotor failures, blade strikes, and the inevitable increases in the costs of aviation parts and insurance.

After a suitable amount of mingling and a glass of champagne, we settled at our assigned table for the requisite rubber-chicken dinner, followed by speeches and awards. Drake handled his portion of it marvelously with a winning smile and a heartfelt thanks. I think I actually glowed with pride.

"Can we escape?" he whispered in my ear when he came back from his trip to the podium.

We excused ourselves and ducked out to a balcony for some air. I kicked off my torturous heels with a sigh of relief.

"Quite a shindig," Drake said, loosening his tie.

"How do you keep track of all these people?"

He grinned. "Years of practice. But it has its perks."

Before I could ask what he meant, a booming voice called out, "Drake, my friend!"

A tall man with artfully tousled salt-and-pepper hair strode toward us, his smile as bright as a searchlight. He wore a several-thousand-dollar suit and a pinky ring with an impressive diamond. I pegged him immediately as the kind of guy who could sell ice to an Eskimo.

"John!" Drake greeted him warmly. "Charlie, meet John Flick. John, my wife, Charlie Parker."

John took my hand, brushing his lips across my knuckles. "Enchanted."

Little over the top. I smiled and resisted the urge to wipe my hand on my dress. But I did slip my shoes back on.

"John owns Flick Helicopters," Drake explained. "Biggest operator on the Gulf coast."

John's laugh was as polished as his shoes. He waved another man over—tall, blonde hair cut short, blue eyes. "Meet my general manager and chief pilot, Harrison Stoker."

Stoker stepped forward and gave us each a firm handshake and winning smile.

"Good to meet you," Drake said.

John took over again. "We're busier than ever, aren't we, Harrison? Just ordered two new H-145s from the Airbus rep this week. Best machine there is for the kind of winds we get over the oil rigs out there offshore. You two should visit Galveston sometime. I'll show you the sights."

They'd barely gotten into memory lane, rehashing the times when they'd worked the same jobs in the early days, when John's phone buzzed. He glanced at the screen, his face darkening. "Excuse me, I need to take this." As he stepped away, Drake and I exchanged glances.

John returned a few minutes later, his earlier joviality replaced by a tense frown. He ran a hand through his tousled hair, mussing it even more, turning to Stoker.

"Everything okay?" his chief pilot asked, concern lacing his voice.

John shook his head. "Still nothing."

Stoker excused himself, saying he would make some calls.

John sighed heavily, addressing Drake again. "We've got a missing vehicle, one of our utility vans. That was Serena, my admin assistant, reporting that there's still no sign of it. Or my mechanic, for that matter. It's been two weeks now."

"Do I know the mechanic?" Drake asked, concerned. The helicopter world is sort of a small one.

John nodded. "I think you might. Benjamin Estevez. I sent him on a short trip to Dallas in the van. Neither he nor the vehicle ever came back. I'm starting to wonder if he might have stolen it."

"Have you reported this to the police?" I asked.

John waved a hand dismissively. "They weren't much help. Said stolen vehicles are a dime a dozen these days. Chances of recovery are slim to none."

"What about your insurance company?"

"Ah, well," John hesitated, "it's an older vehicle, not worth much. I'd rather not involve the insurance folks if I can help it. My premiums are outrageous enough as it is."

I sent a look toward Drake, but he was nodding in agreement. This was getting more interesting by the minute.

"Say, Charlie," John leaned in, his voice lowering conspiratorially, "did I hear that you're in the investigation business—RJP Investigations, right? Any chance you'd be willing to take on this case—find my van and my wayward mechanic?"

I raised an eyebrow. "I thought you said the police were handling it."

John had the grace to look sheepish. "As I mentioned, they're not exactly making it a priority. I'd feel better knowing someone capable was on the job. I'll be in Albuquerque for a few more days. Perhaps we could meet to discuss the details?"

He fished a business card from his pocket and pressed it into my hand. I glanced at Drake, who gave me a slight nod.

"I'd have to check with my partner, see what his schedule is like, but we'll think about it," I said, slipping the card into my evening bag.

John gave a tight grin. "That's all I ask. Now, if you'll excuse me, I should track down Harrison and see if he's learned anything more. Enjoy the rest of the evening!"

As John melted back into the crowd, I turned to Drake. "Well, that was interesting."

Drake nodded, his expression thoughtful. "I'm betting he never even reported the theft. Something about the story is off."

We mingled for another few minutes, but I felt distracted. Something about John's story nagged at me, like a splinter just under the skin.

As we drove away from downtown, I voiced my thoughts. "What do you make of all this, Drake? A missing van, a vanished mechanic, and John's reluctance to involve his insurance company?"

Drake's hands tightened slightly on the steering wheel. "Honestly? It doesn't sit right with me. I've known John for years, worked with him back in Florida before he started his own outfit. He's always been one to cut corners, push the limits of what's safe or legal. That's exactly why I wouldn't go to work for him when he started his own operation. Plus, flying tours in Hawaii held a lot more appeal."

"And I'm glad it did." On one of his tour flights was where we met. I turned to face him. "You never mentioned that John had offered you a job before."

Drake shrugged. "It never came up. But yeah, John's always wanting good pilots. He's got a big operation and a lot of turnover. But he's always been more concerned with the bottom line than following regulations to the letter. It's exactly opposite to the way I run my own business."

"You think he's involved in something shady?"

"I wouldn't put it past him," Drake admitted. "The helicopter business is tough, Charlie. You know that the margins are razor-thin, and the competition is fierce. It's notoriously difficult to get rich in this game, despite what John's flashy lifestyle might suggest."

I mulled this over, pieces of a puzzle I couldn't quite see starting to form in my mind. "So you think there's more to this missing van than John's letting on?"

Drake nodded slowly. "I'd bet money on it. Just ... be careful if you decide to take this case, okay? John can be charming, but he's got a mean streak when things don't go his way. It wouldn't be the first time he pissed off an employee who took revenge in some form."

I reached over and squeezed his hand. "I will. And hey, with you watching my back, what could go wrong?"

Drake chuckled, but I could see the worry lingering in his eyes. "Famous last words, Charlie. Be careful."

As we pulled into our driveway, I gathered my wrap

and purse. Freckles greeted us at the door, her fluffy tail wagging furiously. I knelt to scratch behind her ears, my mind still churning with the events of the evening.

"I'm going to suggest to Ron that we meet with John. It could be an interesting case," I mentioned as Drake hung up his jacket.

He turned to me, a resigned smile on his face. "I knew you would. Just promise you'll keep me in the loop."

I slipped off my shoes again, pulling him into a hug. "Always."

As I lay in bed that night, listening to Drake's steady breathing beside me, I couldn't help but feel a familiar thrill of excitement. I agreed with Drake on this one, and something told me that we'd find more than a simple case of auto theft.

As I drifted off to sleep, John Flick's worried face and Drake's warning echoed in my mind. Whatever was going on with that missing van, I felt sure we could get to the bottom of it. For now, I let the gentle rhythm of Drake's breathing and Freckles' soft snores lull me into a fitful sleep.

Chapter 2

It had been two weeks since he'd jacked the van in Dallas, two weeks of lying low and dodging shadows. For the first seven days, he'd hidden the van in an abandoned garage, then gone about his normal routine so he wouldn't attract attention. The contents of the vehicle had shocked him and he wasn't quite sure what to do about it at first.

Now, finally, he was making his move. The contraband was stashed in the van's side panels, just waiting for the right moment for him to retrieve it and make himself a wealthy man. There was a buyer lined up in New Mexico, but first he had to be sure the setup wasn't a sting operation. No way was Georgie-boy going down for somebody else's crime. All he needed was a decoy, a way to throw any pursuing eyes off his trail.

A little way outside Lubbock, he spotted them—two figures with backpacks, standing on the roadside, thumbs out, hope plain on their young faces.

Perfect, Georgie thought, a slow grin spreading across his face. He eased the van onto the shoulder, gravel crunching under the tires.

The couple approached eagerly, the guy tall and lanky with tattoos snaking up his arms, the girl petite with a shock of short red hair. They looked barely old enough to buy a beer, and he wondered what they were doing out here on their own. Runaways, probably.

Georgie leaned across the passenger seat, fixing what he hoped was a friendly smile on his face. "Where you folks headed?"

The guy spoke first, his voice carrying a surfer's lazy drawl. "Vegas, man. That is, if you're going that way?"

Georgie made a show of considering. "Well now, ain't that a coincidence. I'm headed to Albuquerque myself, visiting my cousin. That's on the way to Vegas, ain't it?"

The girl nodded eagerly, her green eyes bright with relief. "It sure is! We'd be so grateful for a ride, even if it's just part of the way."

"Well then, hop on in," Georgie said, unlocking the doors. "Name's George Lafarge, but folks call me Georgie."

The couple tossed their packs into the back and clambered in, the guy taking the passenger seat while the girl settled in the back among the backpacks and some scattered tools.

"I'm Rory," the guy said, offering a tattooed hand. "And that's my girl, Chelsea."

Georgie shook Rory's hand, noting the kid's firm grip. Probably fancied himself tough. "Nice to meet ya both. So, what brings a couple of young folks like yourselves out to these parts?"

As he pulled back onto the highway, Georgie listened with half an ear as Rory launched into their story.

"Well, see, we're from San Diego originally," Rory began, his hands gesturing as he spoke. "But man, things got pretty heavy back there, you know? Our folks, they just don't get us, always trying to run our lives and shit."

Chelsea piped up from the back, her voice softer but with an edge of defiance. "Mine think Rory's a bad influence. Just because he skipped out on going to college and has a few tattoos."

Georgie grunted noncommittally, his mind racing. These kids were perfect—young, naive, and clearly running from something. If he played this right, they'd transport his cargo, and if the law came looking for them, these two would be the ideal fall guys.

"So we figured, why not see the country, you know?" Rory continued, oblivious to Georgie's scheming. "Make some memories, find ourselves. We saw nearly all of Texas, but you know, Vegas seemed like more fun."

"That right?" Georgie said, feigning interest. "And what you planning to do once you get there?"

Chelsea leaned forward, her face appearing between the front seats. "I can work as a waitress. Figure I can pick up some shifts in one of those big casinos, maybe work my way up to dealing cards. I hear the tips are awesome."

Rory nodded enthusiastically. "And I've got mad skills with computers, man. Bet I could score a sweet gig in IT or something."

Georgie suppressed a snort. And people said *he* wasn't the brightest bulb. These kids were living in a fantasy world, but that suited him just fine. The more unrealistic their plans, the less likely they were to bail on him before he was ready.

"Sounds like you got it all figured out," he said, laying the encouragement on thick. "You're brave, striking out on your own like this. Reminds me of myself at your age."

The lie came easily to Georgie's lips. At their age, he'd already been running numbers for the Dixie Mafia, any thoughts of a straight life long since abandoned. He'd also seen most of Texas, everything from the seedy little beer joints in the has-been small towns to the grimy big cities where you didn't score diddly squat if you didn't already have oil money backing you. By the time he'd turned fifty-five, he was sick of it all. For the last two years, he'd hung around street corners in the warehouse district of Dallas, watching for a chance to score something big. And now he had.

But these kids didn't need to know that.

As the miles rolled by, Georgie let Rory and Chelsea do most of the talking, offering just enough of his fabricated backstory about the cousin in Albuquerque to keep them from getting suspicious. All the while, his mind worked furiously, planning his next move.

He needed to ditch the van soon—it was too hot, too easily traced back to the cartel. But first, he had to figure out a way so's they took the fall if things went south.

The sun was sinking toward the horizon when Georgie spotted a rundown motel on the outskirts of a small town called Muleshoe. Perfect.

"Hey, you kids mind if we stop for the night?" he asked, already signaling to turn. "Been driving all day, and these old bones need a rest."

Rory and Chelsea exchanged a glance, a silent conversation passing between them.

"Sure, man," Rory said finally. "But, uh, we're a little short on cash. Mind if we crash in the van?"

Georgie waved a hand magnanimously. "Nonsense. I'll spring for a room for you two. Least I can do for the company."

As he paid for two rooms at the motel office, Georgie could hardly believe his luck. These kids were practically gift-wrapping themselves for him.

Back at the van, he handed their backpacks out to them and made a show of grabbing an overnight bag for himself. "You two go on and get settled. I'm gonna have a nightcap at the bar next door. You want anything?"

They declined politely, and Georgie watched as they headed to their room, Rory's arm slung casually over Chelsea's shoulders. Young love, he thought with a mixture of contempt and something almost like envy. What a waste.

He was so close now, so close to finally breaking free from life on the streets of Dallas. Just a little longer, and he'd seal the deal with his contact, and then he'd be home free.

Georgie made his way to the bar next door, ordered a whiskey, and settled in to wait. He knew how to read people, a skill he was proud of. And these two were the perfect combination of naïve and slightly dishonest. He'd planted just enough doubt in their minds, just enough clues, to make them take the bait, do the driving on the dangerous leg of the trip.

As he nursed his drink, Georgie's mind wandered back to the day he'd jacked the van in Dallas. Tired of grifting and small con jobs, living in a rat-trap weekly-rate motel, he'd been watching for a chance to score big. He knew the yellow van was being used for something sneaky; maybe cash deliveries were being channeled through Dallas, down to the coast. He'd seen the van come and go, week after week. And that day, he pounced.

But he hadn't counted on the cartel connection. Hadn't expected the heat that came down after he'd taken out that mechanic, Ben what's-his-name. It was supposed to be a simple snatch and grab, but it had spiraled out of control faster than he could blink. Mexicans coming at him from all directions.

Now here he was, weeks later, still running. Unbidden, a scene flashed through his head. One of his mother's many boyfriends, commenting to her that the kid wasn't smart enough to add up two-plus-two. Georgie was thirteen at the time, and the insult stung to his core. He never bragged about making the best grades or anything, but he wasn't *that* stupid. He later told his mother he was glad the boyfriend had taken off with another woman (in fact, the man had *accidentally* fallen down a flight of stairs, Georgie knew for a fact). Mama and Georgie deserved better than that creep. He had street smarts, he bragged. Could smell a good deal a mile away. So, okay, he hadn't yet hit upon a big score, and this particular job was taking a lot longer than he'd ever imagined, and maybe, just maybe wasn't quite going to plan.

He sat up straighter on his barstool, banishing those ideas. No, sir. Georgie Lafarge was about to pull off the score of a lifetime, and these two clueless kids were his ticket to freedom.

He'd heard their whispers when he stopped for gas west of Lubbock. The girl was nervous about him, nervous about how much Rory had told him. She was looking for a way out of their driving arrangement, and he'd played just dumb enough that he knew they would go right along with what he wanted from them.

Across the road, the light in their motel room went out, and Georgie allowed himself a small, triumphant smile. Everything was falling into place.

The cash was still stashed in the van's side panels, along with the drugs he hadn't had time to sell. It was a risk leaving it all there, but he didn't dare carry it with him. The Mexicans knew the van and they knew his face.

An hour ticked by. Georgie nursed his drink, keeping a watchful eye on the motel parking lot through the grimy bar window. Just after midnight, he saw movement. Two figures, unmistakably Rory and Chelsea, crept toward the van with their backpacks in hand.

Georgie held his breath as Rory tried the driver's door, found it unlocked. The interior light flicked on as they climbed inside. He knew the key was where he'd 'accidentally' dropped it near the brake pedal.

There was a long moment of stillness. Georgie could almost imagine their whispered conversation, their moment of decision. Then, the van's engine roared to life. He knew it. By the looks they'd exchanged during the ride, these two had no intention of sticking with him. They wanted wheels of their own.

A grin spread across Georgie's weathered face as he watched the yellow van pull out of the parking lot and disappear down the highway. The bait had been taken, hook, line, and sinker.

Chuckling to himself, Georgie dropped cash on the bar and sauntered out into the muggy Texas night. Phase one of his plan was complete. Now for phase two.

He made his way to the far end of the parking lot, where a beat-up blue Ford pickup sat in the shadows. It was the work of moments to jimmy the lock and hot-wire the engine. As he pulled out onto the highway, Georgie felt a surge of exhilaration. He was back in the game, and this time, he held all the cards.

The kids had a head start, but Georgie wasn't worried. They'd be sticking to the main roads, too green to know any better. He, on the other hand, knew every back road and shortcut in the state. He'd catch up to them soon enough.

Meanwhile, let them unknowingly run interference with the cartel and the cops. Once they reached Albuquerque, he'd show up and take over again—finalize his deal with the guy who'd buy the drugs. Then he'd relieve those kids of the cash and disappear for good. If they got caught in the crossfire, well, that was just tough luck.

As the miles rolled by, Georgie found himself almost feeling sorry for Rory and Chelsea. Almost. They were playing a game they didn't even know the rules to. But that was life, wasn't it? You either played smart or you got played.

The Texas night stretched out before him, dark and full of promise. And danger. Always danger. But Georgie Lafarge was ready for it. He'd been running his whole life, always one step ahead of disaster. This time would be no different.

As the first hints of dawn began to lighten the eastern sky, Georgie spotted a flash of yellow in the distance. A slow, predatory smile spread across his face. There they were, his unwitting pawns, racing toward Vegas and what they thought was freedom.

Little did they know, Georgie would be there every

step of the way, lurking in the shadows, waiting for his moment to strike. He eased off the accelerator, allowing the distance between him and the van to grow. No need to spook them now. He had all the time in the world.

After all, the best cons were the ones where the marks never even knew they'd been played.

Chapter 3

I arrived at the office early, pulling down the long driveway to the parking area behind our converted gray and white Victorian, noting that I was the first one here this morning. Freckles hopped out of the back seat and began her daily sniff-over of the property, making sure no wayward squirrels or roaming cats had disturbed anything. I grabbed my laptop case and called out to her when I reached the back door.

By the time the coffee was ready, I spotted Sally's minivan. She carried a box from Funtime Donuts, a treat neither Freckles nor I would be able to resist. Sally is our part-time receptionist, mommy of two, wife of Ross, who spends her mornings managing our schedules and handling the bits and pieces of what it takes to run a private investigation business. On the weekends, she and her brood are usually out to the woods somewhere.

"I smell coffee." She set the pastries on the table. I had already pulled her favorite mug from the cupboard and poured for both of us.

We doctored our beverages and headed toward her desk, where she offloaded a monster handbag. "Did you guys have a great time at that party last night?"

"The gala was done up big, the meal was average, and Drake gave a humble speech when he received his award. And, we may have a new client."

She raised an eyebrow and stuffed the handbag under her desk.

"A guy Drake knew a lot of years ago. One of his company vehicles is missing, most likely stolen."

"Won't the pol—?"

"He says they're not pushing to find it. I get the distinct feeling he's more worried about whatever is inside the van than the vehicle itself. Anyway, maybe Ron can work his magic on the computer and find something for us to go on. It'd be an easy finder's fee, at the very least." I gave her Flick's business card and she promised to schedule him right away if he actually called.

And with that, I carried my maple glazed donut, coffee mug, and messenger bag upstairs to my office. I had some invoices to enter into the system, and if we never heard from John Flick, I planned to get out of here early and have lunch with an old friend. Linda Casper and I hadn't touched base in months.

However, luck wasn't on my side in that regard. Flick's call was the first one of the morning, and Sally buzzed me to say she'd made an appointment for him to come in at nine o'clock.

Ron arrived with fifteen minutes to spare, during which I outlined the basics of what I thought Flick was going to tell us. He settled at his desk and I stared at the long shadows across the worn wooden floors of the reception area below, absently scratching Freckles behind the ears as I watched my brother drum his fingers on a stack of printed reports.

"Why do we want this case, Charlie?" Ron said, not for the first time. "You said Drake doesn't trust the guy?"

I sighed, adjusting my ponytail band. "Somewhat. But they haven't been in contact for a lot of years. Besides, it's just a missing van and a wayward employee. What could go wrong?"

Ron shot me a look that said he could think of about a million things. Before he could start listing them, the opening of the front door announced our client's arrival.

"Showtime," I muttered, straightening up and tugging at my jeans. Freckles let out a soft woof, clearly picking up on the tension in the room as Sally buzzed my office on the intercom to announce our new client.

Moments later, we walked downstairs to be greeted by John Flick's thousand-dollar suit and megawatt smile. "Charlie, Ron, good morning!" he boomed, shaking hands with both of us. "I can't tell you how much I appreciate your taking the time to meet with me."

I gestured toward the leather chairs around the table in the conference room. "Have a seat, John. Let's talk about your case."

As Flick settled in, I couldn't help but notice the way his eyes darted around the room, taking in every detail. It was a habit I recognized from years of watching suspects and clients alike. John Flick was a man used to sizing up his surroundings, always on the lookout for an angle.

"So," I began, leaning back in my chair, notepad at the ready, "why don't you start from the beginning? Tell us everything you can about the missing van and your mechanic."

John's concern seemed genuine. "Of course, of course. It was about two weeks ago. I sent Ben—my mechanic, Benjamin Estevez—on a routine parts run to Dallas. Simple job, you know? Something we did nearly every week. Pick up some specialized helicopter components, maybe a day's drive there and back."

He paused, running a hand through his artfully tousled hair. "But Ben never came back. Neither did the van. I've repeatedly tried calling his cell, but it just goes straight to voicemail. No response to my voice messages or texts. It's like they both vanished into thin air."

Ron, who had taken up a position leaning against the doorframe, spoke up. "And you're sure Estevez didn't just decide to take an unscheduled vacation? Maybe joy-ride in the company van?"

John shook his head vehemently. "No, no. Ben's been with me for years. He's always been very dependable. This isn't like him at all."

I exchanged a glance with Ron. "John," I said carefully, "have you considered the possibility that Ben might have stolen the van? Maybe he saw an opportunity and took it?"

For a moment, something dark flashed across John's face, there and gone so quickly I almost thought I'd imagined it. Then his affable mask was back in place. "I suppose it's possible," he admitted reluctantly. "But I just can't believe it. I pay Ben very well. His personal vehicle is worth way more than that old van, a high-end SUV he left behind at the office. And even if he did … well, I'm more concerned about getting my van back than punishing Ben."

Ron took a seat at the table. "The van must be pretty valuable for you to go to all this trouble."

John shifted in his seat. "It's … it's not so much the van itself. It's what was in it. Some of those helicopter parts I mentioned are extremely expensive. Special equipment made for my fleet. Without them, I've got birds grounded, costing me thousands every day they're not in the air."

I nodded slowly. That much was probably true. Handling the accounting work for Drake's business, I knew a little something about the cost of parts. Little items could run into the tens of thousands. "All right, John. Can you give us a detailed description of the van? Make, model, color, any distinguishing features?"

As John rattled off the details—a yellow 2015 Ford Econoline, Texas plates, a small dent in the rear bumper—I jotted everything down in my notebook. Out of the corner of my eye, I saw Ron doing the same.

"I'll have my office send over the VIN and registration details," John added. "Anything else you need, just ask. I want this resolved as quickly as possible."

Ron set down his pen, fixing John with a steady gaze. "One thing is bothering me about all this, Mr. Flick. Why aren't the police actively involved?"

There it was again, that flicker of … something … in his eyes. "Ah, well, you see … I thought it best to handle this privately. The police, they have so many cases, you know? I didn't want to bother them with what might just be a misunderstanding."

Ron and I exchanged another look. This time, we were definitely on the same page. Something about this case stank to high heaven.

"John," I said, keeping my voice neutral, "I have to advise you that it's always best to report vehicle theft to the authorities. It can help with insurance claims, and if the van is spotted, the police will be able to act immediately."

John waved a hand dismissively. "I'd rather keep this quiet, if possible. Bad for business, you understand."

I nodded slowly, my mind racing. What kind of businessman doesn't care about a stolen vehicle and potentially thousands of dollars worth of parts? And the liability if a company vehicle were involved in an accident? What was he really hiding?

"All right, Mr. Flick," Ron said, standing up. "We'll take your case." He quoted our standard daily rate, plus expenses. "We'll need a retainer of $2,000 to start."

John's smile widened as he reached for his wallet. "Excellent! I knew I could count on you. Here," he said, pulling out a thick wad of cash. "Five thousand. Consider it a bonus if you can resolve this quickly and … discreetly."

As I accepted the money and wrote out a receipt, trying not to show my surprise at the amount, I couldn't shake the feeling that there was a lot more to this than a simple missing vehicle case.

After John left, promising again to send the additional details about the van, Ron turned to me with a grimace. "I don't really like this guy, Charlie. The story is total b.s."

I sighed, slumping back into my chair. "I know, I know. But we've dealt with some iffy clients before." Like the last one, who definitely had ulterior motives for having us locate his supposedly-dead wife. "And five grand is five grand."

"Unless we get a lead on the van in the next five minutes

and have to refund most of the retainer." Ron shook his head. "It's not just that. Didn't you think it was weird how he kept emphasizing the van's contents? And that bit about not reporting it to the police?"

"I know, right? Talking to Drake last night, John made it sound like he had reported the theft but the police told him not to get his hopes up because there are way too many stolen vehicles to keep track of," I told him, standing up and gathering my notepad and pen.

"All right, let's do some digging. I've got a little time this week, but you do remember that I'm up to my earlobes in work for Borkin, right? I'll run the van plates through the Texas DMV if you'll start looking into Benjamin Estevez, see what we can learn about him." Ron was already heading upstairs for his computer. "And Charlie, remember to be careful."

I gave him a look as I followed. "Ron. I didn't just start this career yesterday."

In fact, it wasn't my choice of career at all, I reminded myself as I walked into my office and let Freckles out of her crate, where I'd bribed her to go when the client arrived. I really just joined this venture with the idea of doing the bookkeeping. But I had to admit that I'd been able to help friends on a number of occasions, the part of the job that felt rewarding. And there really was a particular thrill to catching a bad guy and solving a mystery.

I sat down at my desk and booted up my computer. Within minutes I'd jumped on a couple social media platforms and found guys named Ben Estevez. Several of them.

"Charlie," Ron called from his desk about fifteen minutes later, his voice tight. "You're gonna want to see this. At least it appears he wasn't lying to us this morning. He really never did report the theft of the van, or the disappearance of the mechanic."

I walked across the hall to his office and he turned his screen to show me. Although the government form was a little convoluted to read, he'd highlighted the area he wanted me to see. Okay.

I straightened up, pacing the old floorboards as I tried to make sense of it all. "So, a helicopter operator comes to us, spinning a tale about his stolen van and missing mechanic, but despite what he told Drake and me last night, he never actually reported anything to the authorities. Why?"

"Maybe he's trying to avoid police scrutiny," Ron suggested. "You thinking what I'm thinking?"

I nodded grimly. "He desperately wants the van back. And, I'm thinking that whatever was in that van, it wasn't just helicopter parts. It was something he wouldn't want the police knowing about."

"Bingo," Ron said. "Question is, what was it?"

I ran a hand down the side of my face, frustration mounting. "And where does the missing mechanic fit into all this? Is he a victim, a traitor, or an accomplice?"

Ron shrugged. "Your guess is as good as mine, sis. But one thing's for sure — this is probably a police matter."

I took a deep breath. "Maybe, but we don't know that yet. Shouldn't we take the client at face value and just try to get his van back for him?"

"Maybe we should just give Flick his money back and wash our hands of the whole thing. I don't like the fact that you're mainly on your own with this one, Charlie. Beyond some basic computer searches, I don't have the time."

For a moment, I was tempted. It would certainly be the

easier option. But then I thought of the missing mechanic, Benjamin Estevez. If he was in trouble, didn't we have an obligation to help?

"Let's give it little more effort," I said finally. "We took this case, and we may find that there's a simple answer. But," I added, seeing Ron's worried expression, "I'll be careful. And the moment I discover anything that might backfire on us, we call in the cops. Deal?"

Ron sighed, but I could see the resignation in his eyes. He knew me too well to think I'd back down now. "Deal. But, Charlie, go carefully."

"Let's at least do a background check on Estevez and see what we come up with."

"Okay, I'll get on it. Flick's company records should give me the info I need. Could be we'll discover a criminal record that Flick knows nothing about." He turned back to his monitor and keyboard.

Ron could be right about that—the mechanic could be doing something our client was unaware of. But Drake's words came back to me—his old buddy had been known to flaunt the rules in the past. Anyway, whatever had really happened to that van and its mysterious cargo, we were going to get to the bottom of it. And maybe, just maybe, we'd find one or both of these men were up to something. I shook my head. Why would Flick have hired us to look for the van if he was in on it, if he knew the reason it disappeared.

"Ron, one other thing. I had plans to get together with Linda for lunch …"

"Go. I don't see a huge urgency on the van thing at the moment. By the time you get back, I should have some info on the mechanic and whether he has a record."

I sent a smile in his direction and texted my friend Linda to see if we were still on for lunch. But her return message wasn't so good. Her father had just been sent to the hospital and she was on her way there now. I sent wishes for a good outcome and a few emoji hugs, then went to help dig up information on both John Flick and Benjamin Estevez.

With the lunch plan indefinitely on hold, I decided to be a good girl and have one of the lean meals we always seemed to have in the freezer here at the office. It was on its third minute in the microwave when my phone buzzed inside my pocket.

Dottie. I held my breath. Calls from Elsa's caregiver were rare.

Chapter 4

The sun beat down mercilessly on the dusty yellow van, its newly bashed front fender mocking her. How had she not spotted that big rock when she steered off the road? Chelsea Brown squinted against the glare, her short red hair plastered to her forehead with sweat. She would give anything for a shower right now. She watched, picking at the peeling logo on the side of the vehicle, as Rory fiddled with the engine for the umpteenth time, his tattooed arms streaked with grease and his face set in a mask of frustration.

"Any luck?" she called, already knowing the answer.

Rory slammed the hood shut, wiping his hands on his already filthy jeans. "Nada. This thing's deader than disco." The can of carburetor fluid he'd picked up at the dollar store this morning clearly was not the thing to fix the problem.

Chelsea sighed, leaning back against the sun-warmed metal of the van. They'd barely made it to the outskirts of Santa Rosa before the engine had started sputtering and coughing like an old man with a bad cold. By some miracle, they'd managed to coast into this field on the eastern edge of town, coming to rest near some weathered mobile homes.

That had been three days ago. Three long, sweltering days of indecision and mounting fear.

"What are we going to do, Rory?" Chelsea asked, her voice small against the vast New Mexico sky.

Rory ran a hand through his disheveled hair, leaving a streak of grease across his forehead. "I don't know, Chels. I really don't know."

They'd been asking themselves that same question ever since they'd made their impulsive decision to "borrow" the van from that sketchy guy, Georgie. She remembered his stringy brown hair and those cold, blue eyes. His shabby jeans and ratty t-shirt, and the grime under his fingernails. The man had creeped her out from the moment they got in with him and it had seemed like such a stroke of luck that night at the motel—a free ride, keys left conveniently inside. But now, stranded in the middle of nowhere with a dead vehicle and a whole lot of trouble, Chelsea was beginning to think it was the worst decision of their young lives.

And that was before they'd found the drugs and the money.

Chelsea's mind wandered back to that first night in Santa Rosa, when they'd decided to thoroughly search the van for anything useful. She'd been the one to find the hidden compartment behind a panel in the back.

"Rory," she'd whispered, her heart pounding. "You need to see this."

He'd crawled over, his eyes widening as she pulled out bundle after bundle of tightly wrapped pills. Even in the dim glow of their flashlight, the sheer quantity was staggering.

"Holy shit," Rory had breathed. "Is that what I think it is?"

Chelsea had nodded grimly. "Drugs. A lot of them."

But the surprises hadn't ended there. Behind the packages of pills, they'd found something else — stacks of cash, more money than either of them had ever seen in their lives.

"What the hell kind of van did we steal?" Rory had asked, his voice a mixture of awe and terror.

Now, three days later, that question still haunted them. They'd spent hours debating what to do, their voices hushed even though their nearest neighbors were a good distance away.

"Let's take the money, get a room, bus tickets … something."

"And what if the cash is marked? We can't spend it," he countered. "Drugs and cash together—not a good thing."

"We at least have to get rid of the drugs," Chelsea had insisted. "If we get caught with that much … Rory, we'd go away for years."

He'd agreed, albeit reluctantly, and they'd hiked toward town tossing the damning contraband into three separate dumpsters behind businesses along the way. They'd settled into a shady spot beside a pretty little lake, leaning on their backpacks, thinking of camping there, but a bus full of kids showed up. The adults with the group were giving them the stink-eye, and Chelsea spotted a sign that warned against overnight camping. Back up the hill, back to the van, they went.

First thing Chelsea did was to check the hidden panel as she stashed their packs. The money—that was harder to let go of. In the end, they'd decided to keep it, dividing the cash between their backpacks. It felt wrong, dirty even, but Chelsea couldn't deny the allure of finally having some financial security.

"We could start over, for real this time," Rory had said, his eyes gleaming with possibility, despite his earlier declaration that they shouldn't spend any of it. "No more scraping by, no more begging for shifts at crappy diners."

Chelsea wanted to believe him. But the weight of the cash in her backpack felt like a ticking time bomb.

As the sun began to set on their third day in Santa Rosa, casting long shadows across the dusty field, Chelsea's nerves were stretched to the breaking point. Every flash of headlights from the highway made her jump, convinced that at any moment, the police—or worse, whoever that van really belonged to—would come roaring up to arrest them.

"We need to get out of here," she said, breaking the tense silence that had fallen between them. "Tonight. Sleeping in the van a couple nights was taking a big chance. We can't stay with it any longer."

Rory nodded, his usual bravado subdued. "Yeah, you're right. But how? We're in the middle of nowhere, Chels. It's not like we can just call an Uber."

Chelsea chewed her lip, thinking. "We could try

hitchhiking again. Or maybe there's a bus station in town? We have the cash."

"We talked about that."

"I know, but what are the odds anyone would miss a couple hundred?"

Before Rory could respond, a glint of metal caught Chelsea's eye. She froze, her heart leaping into her throat as she realized what it was—a police cruiser, turning slowly onto the dirt road that led to their secluded spot.

"Rory," she hissed, grabbing his arm. "Cops."

His head snapped up, eyes wide with panic. "Shit. Shit, shit, shit. What do we do?"

Chelsea's mind raced. "Act natural. We're just a couple of kids on a road trip, our van broke down. We don't know anything about drugs or money."

Rory nodded, taking a deep breath to compose himself. But as the cruiser drew closer, it became clear that they weren't the target—at least, not yet. The police car pulled up to the nearest mobile home, and an older woman emerged to greet the officer.

Chelsea strained to hear their conversation, catching snatches of words on the breeze.

"... suspicious vehicle ... young couple ... living in the van ..."

Her blood ran cold. Someone had reported them.

"Rory," she whispered urgently. "We need to go. Now."

He nodded, already moving to grab their backpacks, keeping the solid body of the vehicle between that lady's house and themselves. As they prepared to make their escape, Chelsea's foot kicked something small and hard. She looked down to see a plastic rectangle lying in the dust—a driver's license.

Without thinking, she scooped it up, her eyes quickly scanning the details. Benjamin Estevez, the photo showing a man in his mid-thirties with kind eyes and a slight smile. But it was the smear of reddish-brown across one corner that made Chelsea's stomach lurch. Blood.

"Chels, come on!" Rory hissed, already edging toward the back of the field where a line of scraggly trees offered some cover.

In a split-second decision, Chelsea dropped the license into a small gap between the van's seats. Whatever story this Benjamin Estevez had to tell, she didn't want any part of it.

They had just reached the tree line when the sound of an engine made them both freeze. Peering back, Chelsea saw a tow truck rumbling down the dirt road, the police cruiser leading the way.

"They're taking the van," she breathed, a mixture of relief and fresh panic washing over her.

Rory grabbed her hand. "This is our chance. Come on!"

Hand in hand, they plunged deeper into the sparse woods, the weight of their backpacks—and the illegal cash they contained—a constant reminder of the trouble they were in. As they ran, stumbling over roots and ducking under low-hanging branches, Chelsea's mind whirled with questions.

Who was Benjamin Estevez? What had happened to him? And most pressingly, who did that van really belong to?

She had a sinking feeling they'd find out sooner rather than later.

* * *

Chelsea and Rory hiked the back roads and alleyways, avoiding the main streets of Santa Rosa as much as possible. There was a train station, but no sign of passenger service. A few cars sat on a siding, the kind that were loaded with autos on their way to dealerships somewhere. Everything was locked up tight. The town seemed to consist of one main thoroughfare, which a sign indicated was Old Route 66, with side streets branching out. Small businesses, not much traffic. The kind of place where non-locals stood out. Every passing car was a potential threat.

As the night deepened, they found themselves on the western outskirts of town, huddled behind a dilapidated gas station that had clearly seen better days. The neon OPEN sign flickered weakly, casting an eerie glow over the cracked pavement.

"We need a plan," Chelsea said, her voice hoarse from thirst and fear. "We can't just keep running blindly."

Rory nodded, slumping against the faded stucco side of the building. "I know. But what? We're fugitives now, Chels. We stole a van full of drugs and money. And we left so fast our prints are all over the thing. This isn't some joyride gone wrong anymore."

Chelsea closed her eyes, trying to think through the fog of exhaustion and hunger. "Okay, let's break this down. What do we know?"

"We know we're in deep shit," Rory muttered.

She shot him a look. "Not helpful. Come on, seriously."

Rory sighed, running a hand through his hair. "All right, all right. You found a license, so we know the van belonged to someone named Benjamin Estevez. Or at least, he was involved somehow."

Chelsea nodded. "Right. And judging by the blood on his license, something bad happened to him."

"Then there's the drugs and money," Rory continued. "Way too much of both for this to be some small-time operation."

"And don't forget Georgie," Chelsea added. "He's mixed up in this somehow. He practically handed us the van."

Rory's eyes widened. "You don't think ... was he setting us up?"

The possibility hung in the air between them, heavy and ominous. It made a twisted kind of sense—give the hot van to a couple of naive kids, let them take the fall if things went south.

"If he was," Chelsea said slowly, "then he's still out there. He would *not* let this go. He's probably looking for us. Or for the money, at least."

Rory swore under his breath. "So we've got the cops, whoever owns the drugs, and possibly Georgie all after us. Great. Just great."

Chelsea reached out, taking his hand in hers. Despite everything, the familiar warmth of his skin was comforting. "Hey, we're in this together, remember? We'll figure it out."

Rory squeezed her hand, managing a weak smile. "Yeah, together. So what's our next move, *partner* in crime?"

She pondered for a moment, weighing their limited options. "We need to get out of Santa Rosa, that's for sure. But we can't risk public transportation—there'll be cameras, too easy to track."

"Hitchhiking?" Rory suggested.

Chelsea shook her head. "Too dangerous. That's how

we got in with that Georgie creep."

"So what, then? We can't exactly buy a car."

A thought occurred to Chelsea, a memory from her wilder teenage years. "Maybe we don't need to buy one."

Rory raised an eyebrow. "What are you thinking?"

"I had this friend back in San Diego, I watched her once when we, uh … borrowed a car," she said, a hint of her old mischievous spark returning to her eyes.

"Borrowed? You mean stealing," Rory said, but there was no judgment in his voice, only a grudging admiration.

"We did it once already, right?" Chelsea shrugged. "Desperate times, desperate measures. We'll return it when we're done, I promise."

Rory considered for a moment, then nodded. "All right, I'm in. But where do we go once we have wheels?"

That was the million-dollar question. Chelsea bit her lip, thinking hard. They couldn't go back to San Diego— that would be the first place anyone would look for them. They needed somewhere off the grid, somewhere they could lie low and figure out their next move.

"What about your uncle's cabin?" she said suddenly. "The one in Colorado you told me about?"

Rory's eyes lit up. "Uncle Mike's place? Yeah, that could work. It's pretty remote, up in the mountains. And he only uses it during hunting season."

"Perfect," Chelsea said, feeling a glimmer of hope for the first time in days. "We'll head there, regroup, and figure out how to get ourselves out of this mess."

With a plan in place, however tentative, some of the crushing anxiety lifted from Chelsea's shoulders. They weren't out of the woods yet—not by a long shot—but at least now they had a direction.

As they set off in search of a suitable vehicle to *borrow*, Chelsea tamped down the feeling that their troubles were just beginning. The weight of the cash in her backpack seemed to grow heavier with each step, a constant reminder of the danger they were in.

They found an older SUV sitting on a used car lot that was closed for the night. It was plain vanilla white, and unlocked. She glanced at Rory, saw the determination in his eyes and the set of his jaw as he followed her instructions and fiddled with the wires under the dashboard, and she felt a surge of affection. She hoped he would get them out of this. Somehow.

Within five minutes they were on the road, watching for some way to get off the interstate and onto a less-busy road that would take them north. The night stretched out before them, full of shadows and unknowns. But for the first time since this wild, terrifying adventure began, Chelsea felt a flicker of something like excitement. They were outlaws now, for better or worse, in a vehicle no one could connect to them. Still, she couldn't lose the feeling that someone would be coming after the loot they'd found in that stupid van.

Chapter 5

Georgie Lafarge spotted the van before he actually entered Santa Rosa. He'd taken a random selection of farm roads out of Lubbock, crossing into New Mexico near Clovis (where he, brilliantly, ditched the Texas plates on his borrowed pickup truck and grabbed a yellow and red New Mexico replacement), passing through Tucumcari where he struck up a conversation with a truck stop waitress. Through skillful manipulation and a totally bullshit story, he learned that yes, his *niece* and her friend had passed this way three days ago.

Three days! Georgie felt a momentary jolt of panic. He'd fallen farther behind the couple than he'd planned, and now it was already late afternoon. He smiled and ordered his coffee to go.

Okay, he told himself, back in the truck. They were on Interstate 40, at least. And since he knew their goal was Las Vegas, it was likely they'd stay the route until Kingman, Arizona, before they needed to take a different highway toward Sin City. They'd be nearly three states away from where the van was taken, and he really hoped the cartel dudes were still searching the Dallas area for it. But—that wasn't a chance he could take. He needed to catch up with those kids and recover the treasure he knew to be hidden in the back.

Westbound out of Tucumcari, he realized he hadn't gassed up back there at the truck stop. There was no way the quarter tank showing on the gauge would get him to Albuquerque. He exited at Santa Rosa.

And it was on the Old Route 66, heading downhill toward town, that he spotted the van. His heart thumped, as he realized how easily he could have cruised on past and missed it altogether. Then his brain finally engaged with his eyes and he realized the van wasn't driving down the highway—it was on the back of a tow truck.

Change of plan. He dropped in behind and followed, hoping like crazy it would stay local. It did. The tow truck made its way through town and directly to a local field office of the New Mexico State Police. He felt his head begin to pound.

Georgie pulled into the parking lot of a consignment shop across the road and watched in horror as a gate opened and the tow truck drove into what must surely be an impound lot. An eight-foot-tall chain link fence surrounded the property.

The tow truck driver went through the laborious process of off-loading the yellow van and some helpers pushed it into a parking slot against the dark brown stucco building. He saw no sign of the young couple he'd picked up. He supposed the good news was the lack of crime scene tape anywhere on the van. Good news? Seriously, there was no good news at this moment.

He watched as the tow-truck driver chatted for a very long fifteen minutes with a uniformed officer, then walked inside. The driver came out, another fifteen minutes later, with a slip of paper—most likely a receipt. He got into his truck and drove out. The officer pulled the tall gate shut, wrapped a heavy chain through the links, several times, and snapped on a padlock that Georgie could tell at a distance was a good one.

He glanced at the screen on his cell phone and saw it was 4:57 p.m. Precisely at five, a secretarial-looking woman walked out and got into a Toyota sedan in the front parking lot. A minute later, a uniformed officer got into one of the cruisers there. Both left, heading toward the center of town. One cruiser was left in the lot.

It was too light outside to tell whether interior lights remained on, but he would guess the place was staffed around the clock by somebody. And there would be cameras. And that chain and padlock looked daunting.

He went through his options, but quickly figured out a stranger in town who bought a pair of hefty bolt cutters would be remembered. And someone sitting in a pickup truck in front of a consignment store that was just closing … that guy would be remembered too. He supposed there was one bit of good news. He would have time to gas up the blue pickup.

He cruised back into town, finding a gas station two blocks away. While he waited for the fuel to fill the tank, he ignored the No Cell Phones sign and looked up the hours of the State Police field office in Santa Rosa. Things began to look up when he discovered the desk was only manned until ten p.m.

He bought a burger and fries to go, then drove west on 66, verifying that the consignment shop's neon Open sign was now out. An auto parts store next to it still had a few vehicles in the lot. A rundown old motor lodge was obviously out of business, but a newer place called the Best Value Inn seemed open and partially full. Georgie pulled into the lot and drove to the far end of the row of rooms, checking to be sure he could observe the impound lot from here.

The view wasn't ideal but he could see enough to be certain he would know when the lone officer manning the station finally left for the night. He parked in the shade of a sprawling elm, grateful for some relief from the sun, and ate his burger. When nature called, he stepped out and relieved himself against the trunk of the tree, out of view of the motel office.

He checked the time—barely six. With a full belly and his target in sight, he felt his eyelids drooping. Surely it wouldn't hurt to close them for a few minutes. He hadn't slept, other than fits and starts, for several days now. He'd spent a lot of that time lecturing himself about his decision to leave the van under the control of those kids. But considering he'd spotted vehicles, more than once, with Sinaloa license plates, it was a good thing he had. Now he needed to figure out a way past that tall fence with the razor wire, load the cash into his duffle bag, and get the hell out of here.

And if those kids had discovered the cash and taken

off with it … well, he'd make sure they were sorry. Real sorry.

He was getting worked up, and he forced himself to slow his breathing and keep his eyes shut. A little rest. That's all he needed.

When he woke up, the sky was getting light. One glance confirmed the worst. The van was gone.

Chapter 6

The early morning sun was just peeking over the Sandia Mountains as I pulled out of Albuquerque, pointing my Jeep east toward Santa Rosa. Once past Moriarty and the east-mountain communities, the familiar landscape of scrub brush and grassland rolled by, but I barely noticed it, my mind churning with the latest developments in the Flick case.

Ron had called me at an ungodly hour, his voice tight with excitement. "Charlie, we've got a hit on the van. It's been found in Santa Rosa, impounded by the local PD."

I'd been out the door in minutes, thermos of coffee in one hand, case notes in the other before I remembered my promise yesterday afternoon to Dottie. With her phone call, a new responsibility now joined my list of people and things to look out for this week. I activated the hands-free feature on my phone and asked it to call Elsa.

"Hey, Gram, it's me. How's everything going this morning?"

"I'm on my way out to the garden now, to pick the snap peas. Dottie told me you might be over to help."

"Yeah, well … Ron's got me on another mission right now. Depends on how long it takes, but I might be back in time to help this afternoon."

"Charlie, don't worry about it. I've managed the garden on my own for a whole lotta years."

Yes, but she wasn't in her nineties back then. "Pick the peas, but be careful. Don't lean over, no heavy lifting, and get back in the house before the heat sets in."

"Yes, mama," Gram said with a laugh. "By the way, I heard from Dottie last night. With everything that's going on with her daughter, she called to check up on me. Wasn't that sweet?"

It was, I agreed. "Did she sound okay? She was in a panic when she called me at the office yesterday. She's really worried about her daughter and the baby."

"I'd say she was more disgusted than panicky by the time I talked with her. Said she's going to get Tayla's worthless husband back home and make him live up to his responsibilities."

Good luck, I thought. It sounded like the prospect of a third child, and this one a high-risk pregnancy, had freaked out the middle-aged couple. Dottie's son-in-law had done a runner, and Dottie was having none of it.

"It's not helping that Tayla is under orders for complete bedrest, so her job's in jeopardy. And the cost of daycare for the other two kids is apparently outrageous."

"I've heard that." Which was one more very good

reason Drake and I had opted out of having our own.

"Anyway, I miss having Dottie around the house, but I can manage just fine until she gets back."

"You call me if you need anything. Or Ron. He's in town today, and I'll be back tonight."

"I'll be fine. Bye, Charlie."

I'd swear I heard her say something along the lines of "I don't need a babysitter" as she hung up the phone in her kitchen. Okay, that much was true. But I couldn't help but realize that our roles had now reversed and I felt the weight of that responsibility.

Now, as I sped down I-40 toward the rising sun, I brought my thoughts back to the case. Ron had sounded excited that the stolen van was found. Maybe it would be a simple matter of verifying it was the right one, calling John Flick, and letting him make the arrangements to get it back. There was still the matter of the mechanic who had gone missing along with the vehicle. I didn't get the impression he was with it now, so that would be another thing to explain to Flick when I talked to him again.

Two hours and three pit stops later (note to self: maybe ease up on the coffee next time), I pulled into Santa Rosa. I had visited here several times as a teen, when a high school friend invited me along on visits to her grandparents.

I loved their old house with its rock fireplace, sitting on some acreage a couple miles out of town. I could spend an entire Saturday curled up with a book or walking up the pathway to the barns where Susan's grandfather kept chickens, a pig or two, and a dozen barn cats. Suzie, on the other hand, got restless and we'd usually end up either driving her little convertible or walking into town. The grandparents had a long history here, so I got the guided tour many times. Post office, library, courthouse, five-and-dime (when there were still such places), pharmacy (where the old soda fountain was still in place and we always got a sundae). Then there was Park Lake, a fun spot for a dip on a hot summer day, and of course the well-known Blue Hole. Suzie's grandmother had horror stories of that one—people swimming in it and being sucked under by mysterious currents. But by the time I came along they'd installed a grate over the underground river that could draw someone in, and now it was used by scuba divers for certification training.

It was a small town of less than three thousand people, the kind of place where everyone knows everyone else's business, and a stranger stands out. Perfect for my purposes now.

The Santa Rosa Police Department was located in a long building made of local stone that sat next to the historic Guadalupe County courthouse. As I walked in, the air conditioning hit me like a wall, a blessed relief from the hot day that was building up outside.

"Can I help you?" The officer at the front desk eyed me warily, clearly not expecting a stranger in town.

I flashed my most winning smile and handed over my business card. "Charlie Parker, with RJP Investigations in Albuquerque. I'm here about a van that was impounded recently. A yellow Ford Econoline, Texas plates?"

The officer's eyebrows shot up. "Let me get the detective in charge for you."

Detective? For an abandoned vehicle?

A few minutes later, I was ushered into a small office where a harried-looking man in his fifties sat behind a desk piled high with papers. Detective Garcia, according to the nameplate. My card sat on top of the stack of file folders.

"Ms. Parker," he said, gesturing for me to sit. "What's your interest in this van?"

I perched on the edge of the chair, leaning forward slightly. "We've been hired by the owner to locate it. John Flick, of Flick Helicopters in Galveston. I was hoping to negotiate its return."

Garcia's face clouded over. "I'm afraid that's not going to be possible, Ms. Parker. This van is now evidence in an ongoing investigation."

My heart sank, but I kept my face neutral. "May I ask what kind of investigation?"

He studied me for a moment, clearly debating how much to share. Finally, he sighed. "Look, I shouldn't be telling you this, but I know Ron Parker. You're related?"

"He's my brother." We spent a minute or so exchanging enough information so Garcia felt more comfortable with me.

"We found traces of fentanyl in the back of the van. And a bloodstained driver's license belonging to a Benjamin Estevez."

Flick's missing mechanic. "What about Estevez himself?" I asked, trying to keep my voice steady.

Garcia shook his head. "No sign of him. But given the blood and the drugs, we're treating the vehicle as a crime scene."

I sat back, my mind racing. This was way bigger than Flick had let on. "Detective," I said carefully, "my client never mentioned anything about drugs. He told me the van was carrying helicopter parts."

Garcia snorted. "Yeah, well, unless helicopter parts have suddenly become small, white, and highly illegal, I'd say your client was lying to you."

I couldn't argue with that. The question was, how deep did Flick's lies go?

"We found a couple of fentanyl tablets, and traces of the white residue in the back of the van. There's more," Garcia continued. "We found a random hundred-dollar bill in the back. And there were signs that someone had been living in the van recently. A young couple, according to the woman who reported it."

I leaned forward, my interest piqued. "A couple? Not Estevez?"

Garcia shook his head. "No, definitely not Estevez. The witness described them as kids, really. Early twenties at most. Red-haired girl and a tall guy with tattoos."

My mind was whirling, trying to fit these new pieces into the puzzle. Who were these kids? How did they fit into all this?

"And where are they?" I asked.

"They've vanished," Garcia said, spreading his hands. "By the time we got there, the van was abandoned. We've put out an APB, but so far, nothing."

I nodded slowly, processing all this new information. "What happens now?"

"Well, we've turned the van over to the State Police. They kept it inside their locked yard here until late last night. It's at their headquarters in Santa Fe now. They'll do a more thorough forensic analysis." Garcia leaned back in his chair, fixing me with a stern look. "Charlie, I'd caution you to be very careful with this case. Your client appears to be involved in something far more dangerous than what you've described."

I couldn't help but agree. Although I said all the right

things to Garcia, inside I was seething toward John Flick.

As I left the police station, my thoughts were spinning. What had started as a simple missing vehicle case had morphed into a potential drug trafficking and murder investigation. And somewhere out there were two kids who might hold the key to unraveling it all.

I stood in the shade of a mulberry tree outside the station, deciding what to do next. Call Flick and give him a piece of my mind, check in with Ron, stick around Santa Rosa and ask more questions? In the end, I opted to walk across the street and grab some lunch at a small restaurant that looked new.

Café Espresso sat in the spot where I thought the five-and-dime store used to be, with wide windows facing the courthouse. It was a little early for lunch and only one table was occupied. A young waitress told me to take any seat I wanted, and I opted for a table by the windows. The menu consisted of coffees, pastries, sandwiches, and salads. I chose an Asian chicken salad, which would give me plenty of time to chew and think about my next steps.

For some reason I felt uneasy about calling Flick until I knew more, and since the van was now in Santa Fe and the police were looking into the possibility that Benjamin Estevez was dead, I felt I'd better stay out of that. So I placed a call to our office, and Sally told me Ron had gone to the vital records department downtown. I asked her to leave him a message, but then I got impatient and called his cell. It went to voicemail. I gave the basics of the new information. Told him if I didn't hear back from him I'd talk to him when I got home.

Chapter 7

When I didn't hear back from Ron by the time I finished my salad (which was excellent, by the way), I decided to head home. The drive back to Albuquerque seemed to take forever, the monotonous landscape doing nothing to calm my racing thoughts. By the time I pulled into my driveway, the temperature was pushing one-hundred.

Drake was away on an overnight job, a photo shoot for some western-wear designer's upcoming Christmas line, but Freckles greeted me with an enthusiastic bark, her tail wagging so hard her whole body shook.

"Hey, girl," I murmured, bending down to scratch behind her ears. "At least someone's happy to see me."

I walked into the kitchen and poured a tall glass of iced

tea, peering out the window toward Elsa's house. She'd better not be out in the garden, I thought, taking my new role of elder-watchdog seriously. Just to be sure, I stepped out and walked through the break in the hedge between our properties. All was quiet next door, so I tippy-toed back. This time of the afternoon, odds were good she was taking a nap, most likely dozing in her recliner chair with the television tuned to something gossipy.

I grabbed my tea and went to the dining table to go through the mail I'd picked out of our mailbox. Ninety percent junk, which I stacked for the recycling bin. Something that looked like a payment check from one of Drake's customers, and I carried that one to his desk in our little home office.

In the living room, as if on cue, my phone buzzed. Ron's face popped up on the screen.

I went through the details of what I'd learned in Santa Rosa—the van's contraband, the blood-stained driver's license, the witness's report of two young people who were occupying it when it turned up in town. "Please tell me *you* have some good news," I said, collapsing onto my couch.

Ron's sigh came over the line. "It's news—not exactly positive. I spent most of the day on work for Borkin, but while I was downtown I also did some digging into Flick Helicopters. Charlie, this company is sketchy as hell. There are a couple of pending lawsuits, and I've found connections to some pretty unsavory characters in Texas. Without a warrant I can't access Flick's tax records, but something tells me those won't be squeaky clean either."

I groaned, rubbing my temples where a headache was starting to form. "Great. Just great. Sounds like there's a lot more to it than a stolen van and missing employee. We may be in over our heads here."

"You think?" The sarcasm in his voice was palpable. "Charlie, maybe we should consider dropping this case. It's a police matter."

For a moment, I was tempted. We could tell Flick where his van was, give him back most of his retainer, and wash our hands of the whole mess. But then I thought of Benjamin Estevez, whose blood-stained license was now sitting in an evidence locker. And those two kids, out there somewhere. They'd disappeared for a reason. Were they the cause of all this trouble? Or were they victims of it?

"The police seem to be treating each offense and each jurisdiction separately," I said firmly. "Someone has to put it together, Ron. But we're going to be smart about it. First thing tomorrow, we're going to have a long talk with our dear client, Mr. Flick. I think it's time he started telling us the truth."

Ron was quiet for a moment. "All right," he said finally. "But Charlie, be careful. If we don't get answers that make sense, we're dropping him."

"Aren't you the one always telling me to trust my instincts?" I teased, trying to lighten the mood.

"Yeah, well, right now my instincts are screaming that something's really off. Just watch your back, okay?"

I promised I would, then hung up. As I sat there in the growing darkness, Freckles curled up with her head on my lap. It felt obvious that we were standing on the edge of something bigger than we'd been led to believe. Something dangerous.

But that's the thing in our business—sometimes you have to poke the bear to find the truth. And whatever John Flick was hiding, whatever had happened to Benjamin Estevez and those two kids, I was determined to get to the bottom of it.

Later, I decided as I took a shower and finally dragged myself to bed. Tomorrow we'd start getting some real answers.

As I drifted off to sleep, I tried to put the day's findings out of my mind, but couldn't seem to drop the two young people I'd never met but couldn't stop thinking about. Somewhere out there, they held pieces of this puzzle. And somehow, I had to find them before it was too late.

The next morning dawned bright and clear, but I barely noticed the perfect New Mexico sky as I let Freckles out to the back yard. Beyond the hedge separating our yards, I spotted Gram in her garden, checking the fruit and watering the vegetables before the day became too hot. I walked over to check on her but must admit I didn't take in much of the detail she was telling me about the various plants; my mind was too full of the details of this case.

While the dog gobbled her breakfast, I put on jeans and a V-necked shirt and pulled my hair off my neck into a messy bun. Once we were out in my Jeep, I debated breakfast options. The nearest Lota Burger was slightly out of the way for my short trip to the office, but I succumbed to the temptation. Breakfast burritos ought to help everyone's productivity so I ordered three.

I breathed the heady scent of bacon, egg, and green chile as I picked up my order, doing a one-arm wrestle to keep Freckles contained in the back seat, out of reach of the food until I pulled into my parking spot at the office.

"What's that I smell?" Sally said, not looking up from her computer. I placed the foil-wrapped goodie near her elbow and made my way upstairs.

Ron was already there when I peered into his office, his desk covered in printouts and his computer screen flashing with open tabs. I'd forgotten that he had a bunch of employment background checks to conduct for one of our larger clients, in addition to those for the new client, Borkin, plus this latest case.

"Morning, sunshine," I said, dropping the paper bag on his desk. "I brought breakfast burritos."

He grunted in acknowledgment, barely looking up from his screen. "Thanks. I called John Flick. You ready for this meeting?"

I took a deep breath, pulling a burrito for myself from the sack and heading toward my own office. "As ready as I'll ever be."

Ron nodded. "He'll be here in an hour, right after he takes his chief pilot to the airport for his flight back to Houston. Said he was 'eager to hear about our progress.'" The air quotes were audible in his tone.

"I'll bet he is," I muttered. "Maybe we should go over what we know one more time."

For the next hour, we pieced together everything we'd learned so far. Flick's story about the missing van. The traces of fentanyl the police had found inside it. Benjamin Estevez's bloodstained license. The mysterious young couple. Flick Helicopters' questionable financials.

"We're missing some kind of a connection," I said, frustration creeping into my voice. I paced to the bay window in my office and spotted our client getting out of his flashy sports car. "He's here."

Before Ron could respond, the bell over the front door chimed. I wadded up my food wrapper and tossed it in the trash, rinsing my mouth from my water cup. Downstairs, I heard Sally greet Flick and show him into the conference room.

Ron brushed crumbs from his shirt and headed downstairs with me right behind.

John Flick stood there, all expensive suit and megawatt smile. But this time, I wasn't buying the charm.

"Charlie, Ron," he boomed, shaking our hands. "I hope you have good news for me."

I gestured for him to sit, then fixed him with my best no-nonsense stare. "John, we need to talk. And this time, we need you to tell us the truth. The whole truth."

His smile faltered for just a moment before sliding back into place. "Of course, Charlie. I've been nothing but honest with you from the start."

I leaned forward, my voice low and intense. "Really? Then perhaps you'd like to explain why your van, which you claimed was carrying helicopter parts, was found with traces of fentanyl?"

The color drained from Flick's face so fast I thought he might pass out. "What! Where—"

"Your van was located in Santa Rosa, a couple hours east of here. According to a witness, it was being driven by a young couple, but they scattered as soon as the cops showed up. We don't know anything about them, but we do know the police found traces of fentanyl in the back."

Ron leaned forward in his chair. "What were you really using the van for? Not the transport of helicopter parts. That much is clear."

"Your driver ... his license was in the van, John. And there was blood on it." I smacked a file folder down on the table, more for effect than anything else. "As I said, it's time you told us the truth."

"Charlie ... Ron ... I swear it. I have no idea what's going on here. Ben went to pick up parts and should have been back in Galveston later the same day." His tone sounded earnest enough. "Maybe this young couple?

They're druggies and they stole the van from Benny?"

"Was your mechanic involved with drugs?" Ron questioned.

"No! I mean, you can never completely know somebody, but I'd stake my reputation on Ben Estevez. The guy's a top-notch mechanic. All our mechanics and pilots go through random drug tests—it's an FAA requirement."

Ron looked to me for verification. It was true. Drake and I were bound by the same rules, as commercial operators.

"Okay, so Ben may not be a user, but how else do you explain the fentanyl in your company van?"

Flick sat up taller in his chair, his fingers splayed across the table. "I have no explanation. That van has been outside my control for weeks now. Anything could have happened in that amount of time."

That much was true. I took a deep breath. "Okay, okay. Let's all calm down a little. We're just looking for the answers."

"So, where's my van and when do I get it back?"

I told him what I'd been told about it being in the state police impound lot in Santa Fe. He seemed none too happy at having to make the call, but said he would follow up. He stomped out of the office and revved his engine as he left.

"That guy is totally full of it," Ron commented as we watched Flick roar down our quiet residential street.

"Oh yeah. You notice he didn't ask anything about where his employee might be, only the van. And he gives not one whit about those kids who were driving it."

So, what was Flick still hiding?

Chapter 8

Chelsea and Rory crossed the New Mexico-Colorado border as the sky was becoming lighter in the east. Their borrowed Ford SUV, taken from a used car lot on the outskirts of Santa Rosa, was already protesting every mile at highway speed but somehow holding together.

Chelsea had run her phone battery all the way down, searching out roads that would keep them off the interstate highways and as out of sight as possible. Her hands were cramped from gripping the steering wheel so tightly, her eyes gritty with exhaustion. But she didn't dare stop, not until they were safely hidden away in Rory's uncle's cabin, which was somewhere near Trinidad.

Beside her, Rory dozed fitfully, his head lolling against the window. Chelsea envied him his ability to sleep, even if it was a restless slumber. Her own mind was too wired, too full of racing thoughts and worst-case scenarios to even consider closing her eyes.

As they wound their way north, the terrain growing steeper and more rugged with each passing mile, Chelsea found her thoughts drifting back to the van. To Benjamin Estevez's blood-stained license, hidden away in that small crevice. To the drugs they'd disposed of, and the money now weighing down their backpacks.

What had they stumbled into? It was clear now that this was so much bigger than a simple case of hitching a ride with the wrong guy. Georgie was a slimeball, no doubt about that, but she didn't for one minute believe he was smart enough to have engineered the crimes they'd found evidence of. There were darker forces at play here, dangerous people who wouldn't hesitate to hurt them—or worse—if they were caught.

"Rory," she said softly, reaching over to shake his shoulder. "Rory, wake up. I think this is Trinidad up ahead. You need to tell me where to turn."

"Wha—? Okay." He rubbed vigorously at his eyes and slapped his cheek a couple of times. "We go south for a few miles. At Starkville we're looking for a side road that heads toward Fishers Peak."

Chelsea wished she'd known that ahead of time. She had driven right through Starkville. But it wasn't far to backtrack. Within fifteen minutes they were making the turn Rory had described.

"After a few miles, we'll be looking for the turnoff to the cabin. I'm pretty sure I'll recognize it."

Pretty sure. Chelsea bit back a comment. She was too tired to start an argument now.

A sharp bend in the road snapped Chelsea to attention.

She eased off the gas, guiding the old Explorer around the curve with careful precision. The last thing they needed now was to go careening into a ditch.

She nodded, her eyes scanning the roadside. Sure enough, a few minutes later Rory pointed out a narrow turnoff, half-hidden by overgrown bushes. The vehicle's suspension groaned in protest as they bumped onto the rough track.

For what felt like hours but was probably only twenty minutes, they crawled along the winding dirt road. Just when Chelsea was starting to wonder if they'd taken a wrong turn, the trees opened up to reveal a small clearing. And there, nestled against the backdrop of towering pines, stood a rustic log cabin.

"We made it," Rory breathed, a note of relief in his voice. "I remember the blue curtains on the front windows."

Chelsea put the SUV in park and cut the engine, the sudden silence almost deafening after hours of road noise. For a long moment, they just sat there, staring at their sanctuary.

Finally, Chelsea spoke. "What now?"

Rory reached over, taking her hand in his. "Now we rest. Regroup. Figure out our next move."

She nodded, squeezing his hand. "And the money?"

A shadow passed over Rory's face. "We'll deal with that too. But first, sleep. I don't know about you, but I'm dead on my feet."

As if to emphasize his point, he let out a massive yawn. Despite everything, Chelsea found herself smiling. It was such a normal, Rory thing to do, so at odds with the craziness of their situation.

They grabbed their backpacks and made their way to

the cabin. Rory fished the spare key out from under a loose floorboard on the porch, and soon they were inside.

"I need to charge my cell. It died along the way," she told him.

"Ooh, problem there. The place doesn't have electricity."

And you couldn't have thought to tell me this ahead of time?

"There's a generator." Then he looked sheepish. "But we'd better not run it, not until we make sure no one's in the neighboring cabins. We don't want anyone to know we're here."

Well, *yeah*. She heaved a sigh and let it go. For now, they had daylight. After some rest, they'd figure out the rest of it.

The cabin was small but cozy, smelling of pine and old wood smoke. A thick layer of dust covered everything, but Chelsea hardly noticed. All she could focus on was the large bed in the corner, piled high with quilts and looking more inviting than any five-star hotel.

Without bothering to undress, they collapsed onto the bed, dropping their backpacks—and the illicit cash they contained.

Chapter 9

Georgie wanted to kick himself from one end of the county to the other. How could he possibly have slept through it while the van left the impound lot? And worse— who had the money and the stash—those dumb kids or the cops? The fentanyl, in itself, was a huge cash cow that had fallen into his lap. Why hadn't he tracked down some of the dealers in Dallas or Fort Worth and offloaded it right away, instead of heading for Albuquerque?

The questions were endless.

He left the blue pickup where he'd parked all night and walked to a diner a couple blocks away, trying not to let too many people in this podunk town associate him with the truck. His head was splitting. He wasn't used to having so many problems to think through at once. Or maybe it was a lack of caffeine.

Back in Dallas, down in the warehouse district, he'd strolled the streets a lot, and having a cup of coffee in hand made him look more like he had purpose. He pulled a plastic comb from his back pocket and tried to do something respectable with his hair. He wished now that he'd tucked away a few more of the bills from the cash hoard. But hundred-dollar bills created memories, especially when coming from a stranger in a town this size. Better that he pay for his breakfast with a crumpled twenty.

The waitress on the early shift looked like she didn't really want to be there any more than he did, but she handed him a menu laminated in plastic and was ready with the coffee pot right away. He downed half of the hot brew as he decided on two eggs, over-easy, extra bacon, and two slices of white toast. His head settled a little, after the first few sips.

Okay, he thought, where have those damn kids gone? He'd only seen the van and tow truck from a distance, but it didn't appear the couple were with it. Had it broken down and they called for the tow? Nah, that didn't make sense. It would've been taken to a garage instead. Plus, the little turds knew good and well they'd stolen the van from him. Maybe they'd been arrested, the van towed after the cops hauled them off.

But the idea of walking into a police station and asking about them made him feel like he was breaking out in hives. He'd have to give this some more thought.

His bacon and eggs showed up and he attacked the meal with vigor.

Chapter 10

It was late afternoon, the sun casting long shadows across the planks of the cabin floor. Chelsea sat cross-legged on the sagging couch, her fingers absently tracing the frayed edges of a hole in her jeans. Across from her, Rory paced back and forth, his lanky frame taut with nervous energy.

"We can't stay here forever, Chels. Two days and I'm going a little nuts," he said, running a hand through his disheveled hair, a nervous habit. "We need a plan."

He'd been the one to suggest they abandon the stolen vehicle they'd arrived in, wiping it down and leaving it in a parking lot, then hiking back to the cabin, so no one could trace it to them. Chelsea sighed, her gaze drifting to the backpacks stuffed with cash that sat like accusatory sentinels in the corner of the room. The weight of their situation pressed down on both of them.

"I know," she said softly. "But what are our options? We can't exactly waltz into a bank and deposit that money. And we can't keep stealing cars, either."

Rory stopped his pacing, slumping down next to her on the couch. The ancient springs creaked in protest. "Maybe … maybe we should call your parents," he suggested.

Chelsea noticed he said 'your parents' not 'our' parents. Her head snapped up, her green eyes both sad and scared. "Rory, you know we can't do that. Not after what happened."

The memory of that night, when she'd announced she was leaving with Rory, hung between them, unspoken but ever-present. The shouting, the look of betrayal in her mother's eyes. Their profound disappointment in her. She really didn't want to go back there.

Rory reached out, taking her hand in his. His skin was warm, his fingertips calloused from playing the guitar. "I know," he said softly. "I just … I'm worried about you, Chels, about whether I can protect you. This thing is way more than I ever expected it to be."

Chelsea squeezed his hand, trying to draw strength from his touch. "I'm scared too," she admitted. "But we're in this together, right? We'll figure it out."

He nodded, managing a weak smile. "Together. Always."

They sat in silence for a moment, each lost in their own thoughts. The cabin creaked and settled around them, the unfamiliar noises of the forest filtering in through the log walls.

Finally, Chelsea stood up, stretching her stiff muscles. "We need food," she declared. "I can't think straight when I'm this hungry."

Rory's stomach growled in agreement. "Yeah, but where? We're in the middle of nowhere, and we can't risk using that cash in town. And what about the cops? They could be looking, and someone might recognize us."

Chelsea chewed her lip, thinking. They'd been surviving on the canned goods they'd found in the cabin's pantry, but those supplies were running low and cold soup just wasn't appealing anymore. They needed real food, and soon.

"I saw a bar about a mile down the road when we drove in," she said slowly. "Looked a little rough, but it's probably got passable food. Maybe we could use one of the hundreds?"

"Huh-uh. Two people like us with shiny new bills? It'll attract attention."

"Okay, then let's scrape together enough change for a burger?"

Rory looked skeptical. "I don't know, Chels. Sounds risky. What if our faces are on the TV?"

She shrugged, trying to project more confidence than she felt. "Got any better ideas? Besides, we'll blend in better there than at some family restaurant. No one will look twice at a couple of scruffy kids."

After a moment's hesitation, Rory nodded. "All right. But we're careful, okay? In and out, no drawing attention to ourselves."

Chelsea agreed, and they set about gathering what little cash they had left from before their unexpected windfall. Between them, they scraped together just over twenty-five dollars in crumpled bills and loose change.

As they stepped out of the cabin and into the cool mountain air, Chelsea felt a flutter of nervousness in her stomach. They'd been holed up for a while, hiding from the world. Venturing out felt both exhilarating and terrifying.

The walk to the bar took longer than expected, the winding dirt road seeming to stretch on forever. By the time the neon beer signs came into view, the sun had dipped below the horizon, painting the shadows in deep purples and blues.

The bar was a low, squat building with weathered wooden siding and a gravel parking lot filled with motorcycles. A hand-painted sign proclaimed it to be The Rusty Nail. The thump of bass from inside vibrated through the ground, and the smell of cigarette smoke and grilled meat drifted on the air.

Chelsea and Rory exchanged a glance, almost a silent conversation. With a deep breath, they pushed open the screen door and stepped inside.

The interior was dim and hazy, lit mainly by neon beer signs and a few grimy fixtures hanging from the ceiling. The bar was crowded, filled with leather-clad bikers and rough-looking locals. Conversations paused as heads turned to regard the newcomers, curious and not entirely friendly gazes sweeping over them.

Chelsea thought belatedly that she should have brought her phone's charger cord and used this chance to bring it back to life. She cursed under her breath and felt Rory tense beside her, his hand finding hers and squeezing tightly. She squeezed back, trying to project a confidence she didn't feel.

They made their way to the bar, Chelsea's heart pounding so loudly she was sure everyone could hear it over the blaring classic rock. The bartender, a burly man with arms like tree trunks and a ZZ Top beard, eyed them suspiciously.

"What'll it be?" he growled.

Chelsea swallowed hard. "Two burgers and waters, please," she managed, her voice sounding small and young, even to her own ears.

The bartender's eyes narrowed. "You kids old enough to be in here?"

Before Chelsea could stammer out a response, a voice behind them cut in. "They're with me, Joe. Put it on my tab."

They turned to find a mountain of a man grinning down at them, his beard shot through with gray and his leather vest covered in patches.

"I'm Bear," he said, extending a hand the size of a dinner plate. "Welcome to The Rusty Nail."

Rory shook the offered hand, looking like a child next to the massive biker. "Thanks, uh, Bear. I'm Rory, this is Chelsea."

Bear's eyes twinkled with amusement. "You two look like you could use a good meal and a friendly ear. Why don't you join us?" He gestured to a table in the corner where several other bikers sat.

Chelsea hesitated, alarm bells ringing in her head. This wasn't part of the plan. They were supposed to get food and leave, not socialize with a group of intimidating strangers. And *why* did Rory give their real names?

But before she could politely decline, Rory was nodding. "That'd be great, thanks," he said, clearly relieved at the unexpected kindness.

As Bear led them to the table, Chelsea shot Rory a panicked look. He squeezed her hand, trying to reassure her. They were improvising now, walking a dangerous line, she knew.

The next hour passed in a blur of introductions, stories, and the best burger Chelsea had tasted in weeks. Despite her initial fear, she found herself relaxing slightly. The bikers were rough around the edges, sure, but they were also funny and surprisingly welcoming.

But as the night wore on and the beers flowed freely (though Chelsea and Rory stuck to water), the atmosphere began to shift. The jokes got cruder, the laughter louder and more aggressive. Chelsea noticed some of the other patrons eyeing their table with growing hostility.

"So, what brings you kids to our neck of the woods?" a guy named Zeke asked, his words slightly slurred. "You look a little young to be out on your own."

"Just passing through," Rory said, trying to keep his tone casual, improvising answers. "Doing some camping, you know?"

An older biker with a face like weathered leather leaned in, his bloodshot eyes narrowing. "Camping, huh? With what gear? Didn't see no car outside neither."

The friendly atmosphere evaporated in an instant. Chelsea's heart began to race as she realized how suspicious they must look. Although they were both over twenty, to a stranger they looked like two teenagers, clearly out of place, with no visible means of transportation.

"We, uh, we parked a ways back," Rory stammered. "Didn't want to disturb anyone."

The leather-faced biker snorted. "Bull. You two are running from something, ain't ya? What'd you do, knock over a liquor store?"

"Now, now, Spike," Bear rumbled, but there was an edge to his voice now. "No need to go makin' accusations."

But it was too late. The mood had turned ugly, suspicion

and alcohol fueling the undercurrent of aggression. Chelsea saw hands tightening on beer bottles, bodies tensing for confrontation.

"I think we should go," she whispered to Rory, tugging on his sleeve.

He nodded almost imperceptibly, his eyes darting around the room, looking for an escape route.

"Not so fast," Spike growled, reaching out to grab Chelsea's arm, leering at her. "I think maybe we ought to get to know each other a little better first."

Chelsea's first instinct was survival. She twisted out of Spike's grasp, her elbow connecting solidly with his nose. There was a satisfying crunch and a howl of pain.

"Run!" she yelled, giving Rory a shove on the shoulder and bolting for the door.

They burst out into the cool night air, the sounds of chaos erupting behind them. Without pausing to think, they sprinted down the road, feet pounding on the gravel, hearts racing in terror.

They ran until their lungs burned and their legs felt like jelly. When they heard the noisy motorcycles come to life, they dashed off the road and into the thick forest underbrush, running until they were gasping for breath as the Harleys rumbled on into the night.

For several long minutes after the last of the bikes went by, they crouched there in the darkness, listening intently for any sign that someone knew where they were. But there were only the normal sounds of the forest at night—the hoot of an owl, the rustle of small animals in the undergrowth.

As the adrenaline began to fade, the reality of their situation came crashing down. They were alone in the woods, unsure how far away from the cabin, with no food, no transportation, and a group of angry bikers potentially looking for them.

"What do we do now?" Rory whispered, his voice shaky as he stared up into the pitch-dark sky.

Chelsea closed her eyes, fighting back tears of frustration and fear. They'd almost enjoyed the evening—a decent meal, a moment of normalcy. And now they were back to square one, worse off than before.

"We need to keep moving," she said finally, her voice stronger than she felt. But as she stared around in all directions, she realized they didn't know the way back to the cabin. "We'll have to sleep outside or find another place to hole up, at least for tonight."

Rory nodded, his face pale in the scant starlight filtering through the trees. Nothing in his experiences on the track team at school or playing guitar with a dinky garage band had prepared him for this. "And tomorrow, what then?"

Chelsea took a deep breath, squaring her shoulders. "Once it's daylight, we'll figure out our next move. For real this time. No more running blind, no more half-baked plans. We need to decide what we're going to do with that money, and how we're going to get out of this mess. Come on, let's try to sleep a little."

As they scraped up pine needles to make a cushion and spread their jackets over themselves for cover, Chelsea couldn't shake the feeling that they were running out of options—and time. The weight of all their bad decisions pressed down on her like a physical thing.

But at least she wasn't alone. And as long as they had each other, they had a chance. It wasn't much, but it was all they had to hold onto in the darkness. She didn't let Rory see the tears that slid from the corners of her eyes.

As the first hints of dawn began to lighten the sky, Chelsea noted which direction was east. She stretched and slipped away, finding a large shrub to duck behind for a quick pee. Remembering they'd walked northeast from the cabin to the bar, she tried to orient their position. How far had they walked? And how far had they come into the woods, after the scare with the bikers?

They needed to get back to the cabin. All their stuff was there, including the mostly inoperable cell phones and the almost-useless cash. Unlike Rory, she was willing to take small chances with that. But they needed to be smart about it. Needed to carefully think about each move.

They had to. Their lives depended on it.

Chapter 11

W hat really set me back was the way he obviously cared more about the van than his employee, a guy he said had been with him for years." I ranted while Drake unpacked the overnight bag he'd taken on the photo shoot with him.

It was nearly eleven p.m. and my sweet husband looked a little ragged around the edges from two long days of flying. Still, he let me go on.

"Not to mention the young couple who were seen, probably living in the van. Doesn't John Flick care at all about them?"

Drake dropped dirty clothes into the hamper then turned to me, placing his hands on my shoulders and lowered his forehead to touch mine. "I doubt it. Show me any operator who genuinely cares about his employees, enough to move heaven and earth to find them. We're cogs in the wheel, and the bottom line is profit. It's why I quit working for someone else and started my own operation."

I knew this. We'd had the discussion for years. I relaxed against his chest. We ended up in the shower together but were too tired to pursue lusty thoughts any further than that. We snuggled together in bed and I briefly filled him in about Dottie's family emergency and the fact I was now also responsible to check in on Elsa throughout the day. I talked until I realized his breathing had slowed and he was fast asleep.

I lay there with my eyes open for a little while longer. Tomorrow I would pursue the case, focusing on what had happened to Benjamin Estevez and the missing couple whose names I didn't even know yet.

* * *

I woke up still thinking about them and decided I'd make another run to Santa Rosa to ask more questions. Surely, someone could provide information that would lead to the mysterious pair. I couldn't help it—I had a sinking feeling these two were in trouble over the things they must have found in the back of that van. And if John Flick didn't care, well, someone should.

Drake and I were eating breakfast at the dining table and mindlessly staring at the morning news on the TV across the room. The big news—for days now—was about wildfires in Arizona. Drake told me he had already been advised to be on standby. And not two minutes later the phone rang.

"It's Pep," he said, picking up his phone and heading toward his home office where his maps and paperwork were always ready.

My heart did a little flip. Pep Sanchez was Drake's contact at the Forest Service. Less than two minutes passed before Drake was back in the living room, dropping his ready-bag beside the front door.

"They're calling us all out this time. Teams from all over the Southwest are assembling near Holbrook, then they'll dispatch us."

I already knew from the news that there were fairly large fires near Heber and Show Low, with others on the New Mexico side of the border, around Magdalena. To call out small ships like Drake's meant the bigger Sky Cranes and tankers were already being kept busy all day. I rose from the table and asked if I could help him gather anything. Already, I was on my way to the kitchen to put together some sandwiches and snack foods.

We were somewhat used to this drill, but it didn't make it any easier to watch him load his things in his truck. The long hug and kiss were supposed to reassure me that he would return safely. This time, it didn't quite work. Too many other things, too much hung unsettled right now. This felt too real.

Take care of him. I sent up a little prayer as he backed out of the driveway and blew me another kiss.

I turned to see Elsa standing on her front porch, wearing her robe and slippers. Freckles followed me as I walked over to see how she was doing. She'd already figured out where Drake was headed. She's an avid watcher of the newscasts, no matter how depressing they get.

She invited me over for juice and toast, but I honestly

couldn't remember whether I'd left my own refrigerator
door standing open, we'd been in such a rush. I told her I
would stop in before I left for work.

My head felt a little like bursting—filled now with
thoughts of Dottie and her daughter's situation, Gram
alone at home without her caregiver, the missing van and
the young couple who'd been tied to that situation, and
now thinking of Drake hovering above a fire. I walked in
my house and paused to simply breathe for several minutes.

I dressed in my usual jeans and t-shirt—a turquoise
one this time—and performed my short routine to be
ready for work. The kitchen didn't need a lot of cleanup
and Freckles had already been fed. When I walked over
to Gram's, she was dressed in cotton slacks with a cute
matching top and had her sun hat on.

"Don't stay out in the garden too long," I cautioned
her. "It's going to be another hot one today."

"Oh, I know. Cissy the weather girl already told me
about it." She was dutifully smearing sunscreen on her
arms and the backs of her veiny hands.

"I have to drive back to Santa Rosa today, but Ron's
at the office. If you need anything at all, he's less than ten
minutes away."

She gave me an indulgent smile. "I know that, sweetie.
I'll be fine. You'll leave Freckles here with me, won't you?"

Uh. I actually hadn't considered that. Drake was
supposed to be home today. I couldn't very well take the
pup along with me. Leaving her in the car, as hot as it
would be, was not an option.

"Please? She's good company, and she already has
treats and food over here. You know, in case you're gone
a while."

A little nervously, I agreed. I got the dog's leash from home and an extra chewy bone to keep her occupied. And as further insurance, I called Ron before I locked up, letting him know the situation with Elsa. I told him I couldn't stop thinking about the young couple who'd arrived in Santa Rosa in Flick's stolen van, and I wanted to go back and ask more questions, see if I could locate them. He didn't comment on the family or the dog, just cautioned me to be careful on the road.

Once again, the familiar section of I-40 stretched out through Tijeras Canyon and beyond. This time, though, my focus wasn't on John Flick or his mysteriously vanished van. My mind was still consumed with thoughts of the young couple who'd last been seen with it.

Who were they? Where had they come from? And most pressingly, where had they gone?

The blood found in the van and the traces of fentanyl also weighed heavily. From the little I'd heard I didn't think these kids, whoever they were, were hardcore drug dealers. They could be in serious danger. And for reasons I couldn't quite articulate, I felt responsible for finding them.

As I pulled into Santa Rosa for the second time in as many days, I consulted my GPS map to refamiliarize myself with the lay of the land. Cruising through town I spotted many familiar places, but so many things had changed, too. It would be fun to revisit the places Susan and I used to frequent, but I had to remember this trip was business first.

As I drove up the incline toward the neighborhood where the van had been found, I was pleased and surprised to see it was in the same area where my friend's grandparents once lived. It was a quiet area on the outskirts of town, a mix of modest houses and mobile homes. The kind of place where everyone knows everyone else, and the appearance of a stranger stands out. The grandparents' white clapboard home was on the right, still standing back from the highway, although a business had been erected at the edge of the roadway, making the house hard to spot.

A quarter mile farther on, I came to a left-hand turn and spotted the little mobile home community where the police detective told me the van had ended up.

I parked my Jeep and got out, stretching my stiff muscles. June is normally our hottest month, and this morning was going to be one of those.

As I surveyed the area, my eyes were drawn to a tidy mobile home with a meticulously maintained garden. And there, peering out from behind a lacy curtain, was a face that practically screamed "neighborhood watch." Most likely this was the witness Garcia had mentioned.

I made my way up the gravel path, working on my most disarming smile. Before I could even knock, the door swung open.

"Well, it's about time someone came to ask me what I saw," the woman said by way of greeting. She was in her late seventies, with perfectly coiffed white hair and sharp eyes that missed nothing. "I'm Violet Merkle. And you are?"

"Charlie Parker, private investigator," I said, handing her a business card. "I'm looking into the case of that van that was abandoned out here. I was hoping you might have some information."

Violet's eyes lit up like I'd just handed her a winning lottery ticket. "Oh, I've got information all right. Come in, come in. I'll put on some coffee."

She ushered me through a small living room jammed with '70s-era furniture. A yellow tabby cat rubbed against my ankles then meowed loudly and led the way to the kitchen. I took in neatly arranged bookshelves filled mostly with knick-knacks and Bible study materials.

Framed photos gave me the idea Violet had a grown son with a blonde wife and two rather average-looking kids. Based on the clothing, the kids had been little ones about the time Violet moved into this mobile home. Odds were, many of the scattered wallet-sized pictures were grandchildren or greats.

I heard the clink of china and cutlery, and before I knew it, I was seated at a doily-covered table, a cup of strong coffee in front of me. Violet Merkle bustled about, fussing with little things in the kitchen.

"I knew something was off about those two the moment I laid eyes on them," she began, taking the seat across from me and leaning in conspiratorially. "Young people these days, always up to no good. But these two, they were different. Skittish, like they were scared of something."

I nodded encouragingly, jotting notes in my trusty notepad. "Can you describe them for me, Mrs. Merkle?"

"Violet, please," she insisted. "Well, the girl was a tiny little thing, couldn't have been more than five-foot-nothing. Red hair, cut real short. Punk rock style, you know. And the boy, he was tall and lanky, covered in those awful tattoos."

My pen paused. This matched the description I'd gotten from Detective Garcia. "Did you ever speak to them?"

Violet shook her head. "No, they made me a little nervous. And, even though the van died the very minute they drove up here, they kept to themselves. But I saw them coming and going, walking. Always looking over their shoulders, like they expected trouble to follow them. I pictured them as runaways, kids looking for a better situation, probably looking for work in town. They would have needed money to get that van running again."

"How long were they here?" I asked.

"Oh, about three days, I'd say. They were living in that van, you know. They might have walked into town for food, or like I said, looking for jobs. In this heat! I was half tempted to invite them in, offer them a proper bed. But you can't be too careful these days."

I nodded sympathetically, even as my mind raced. Three days. What had they been doing all that time? I could check out the nearest restaurants, places they might have applied for work. With luck, maybe they found jobs and got a place to stay and were still around.

"Did you notice anything else unusual? Any visitors, strange noises?"

Violet's eyes narrowed in concentration. "Well, now that you mention it, there was one thing. One afternoon, I heard raised voices. Like they were arguing about something. I didn't see them that night, and the next day they were gone."

I leaned forward, my interest piqued. "Gone? Just like that?"

"Just like that," Violet confirmed. "I got up to water my zinnias, and noticed the van was all closed up. I had this horrible feeling they might be in there, dead from the heat."

I sat back, processing this information. "Did you walk over and check on that?"

"Oh, no. Not me. Like I said, can't be too careful." She

shifted in her seat. "I called the police department, asked them to check on it."

"Violet," I said carefully, "why did you wait to report the van?"

She had the grace to look slightly embarrassed. "Well, I didn't want to cause trouble if I didn't have to. They seemed like nice kids, just down on their luck. But it was when I didn't see any movement for a whole day, I got worried."

I nodded, understanding. It was a common enough reaction. People often hesitated to get involved, even when they knew something was off.

After thanking Violet for her time (and declining a second cup of coffee), I made my way over to the empty field where the van had been found. The police had long since cleared the scene, but I hoped I might spot something they'd missed.

The area where the van had been parked was just a patch of bare earth now, but I could still make out the tire tracks. I crouched down, examining the ground closely. There were footprints all over the place, some leading away from where the van had been parked. Two sets—one small, likely the girl's, and one larger, probably the boy's.

I followed the tracks as far as I could, my eyes scanning the ground for any clues. They led toward the graveled road that connected with the highway. Backtracking, I saw other tracks leading from the bare spot into a nearby copse of piñon and scrub juniper. As I approached, I caught a strong whiff of urine. Okay, that answered one question about how they were dealing with a basic daily need.

Had they fled on foot? If so, where were they heading? Violet had suggested she thought the kids needed money to get the vehicle running. Was that the reason they left the van behind? Garcia hadn't mentioned it was not operational, but perhaps the police hadn't actually tried to start it, just towed it away.

A mechanical breakdown explained a lot—why they would stay out here for days on end, why they walked to town when they needed anything, and why they finally gave up on driving it away.

Heading back to my Jeep, I spotted Violet Merkle at the window of her double-wide. I sent a smile in her direction, got into my vehicle and started it. With a wave, I pulled away and drove toward town.

Chapter 12

Cruising down the hill, I spotted the turn for Park Lake. It would provide a pleasant, shady spot to pull over and touch base. I stopped under an ancient cottonwood and pulled out my phone. There was a text from Drake, saying he'd arrived safely at the incident command center in Heber and was awaiting instructions. I then hit the button for Ron.

"Tell me you've got something," I said when he picked up.

"Hello to you too, sis," Ron grumbled, but I could hear the rustle of papers in the background. He was hard at work. "I've been combing through missing persons reports from Galveston to Santa Rosa. It's a long shot, but I figured if these kids ran away from home, someone might be looking for them."

"Good idea. Any luck?"

Ron sighed. "Nothing concrete yet. There are a few possibilities, but without more details, it's hard to narrow it down. How about you? Learn anything useful from the local busybody?"

I filled him in on my conversation with Violet and my examination of the scene. "The neighbor never actually spoke with them, so I don't have names for you. She did take a picture—a really awful Polaroid. I'll forward that to you, although it's taken from a distance and not great quality. I'm worried, Ron," I admitted. "These kids could be in real danger."

"I know," he said softly. "We're doing what we can, and we'll just hope for a break."

After hanging up, I stood for a long moment, staring across the peaceful water of the small lake. Playground equipment filled a small area, and picnic tables ringed the southern end of it. A dozen kids were in the water, taking turns on the twisty water slide that dumped them into the lake, eliciting shrieks and shouts.

And somewhere out there, two scared young people were on the run. Based on the evidence Detective Garcia had described, I had to wonder what kind of dangerous secrets they might be harboring. In typical Charlie Parker fashion, I'd taken on the burden of thinking I was their best hope of getting out of this mess alive. Maybe I was.

I found myself trying to piece together their story from the fragments I'd gathered. What had driven them to take the van? Were they willing participants in whatever scheme this was, responsible for whatever had happened to Ben Estevez, or unwitting pawns caught up in something far beyond their understanding?

And what about the argument Violet Merkle had overheard? What could have been so urgent, so divisive, that it drove them to abandon their only shelter and flee into the night?

I made a mental list of next steps. We needed to expand our search, look for any reports of two young people matching their description across a wider area. Ron would continue to work on that, plus dig deeper into John Flick's background and business dealings. Something told me the key to this whole mystery lay in understanding exactly what kind of operation he was really running.

But most pressingly, we needed to find those kids. The blood in the van haunted me. Were they hurt? In danger? Or worse?

My watch told me it was barely past noon, but my body, running on coffee and adrenaline, felt like it had been days since I'd left Albuquerque.

I'd been about to hit the road back home when a thought struck me. Why leave now? The trail was still fresh, and there were plenty more people to talk to in this small town. Someone other than Violet must have seen our mystery couple.

I started my Jeep and headed back out, armed with my notepad and the grainy Polaroid photo Violet had managed to snap of the young couple. It wasn't much—just a blurry shot of two figures near the van—but it was better than nothing. I decided to backtrack to the eastern edge of town, thinking it was most likely the direction from which they had approached, coming from Texas.

My first stop was a gas station-convenience store on the edge of town. It was a longshot, but they may have stopped for gas when they arrived, or maybe they'd walked from Violet's neighborhood up here for snacks or something.

The bell jingled as I pushed open the door, the blast of air conditioning providing a welcome relief from the heat outside. Behind the counter, a middle-aged man with thinning hair and a scraggly beard looked up from his tattered copy of *Car and Driver*.

"Help you?" he drawled.

I introduced myself and showed him the photo. "I'm looking for information on this couple. They were in town a few days ago, driving a yellow van. Ring any bells?"

The man squinted at the photo, then shook his head. "Nah, don't recognize 'em. But Janie might. She works the night shift, sees all sorts come through."

I jotted down Janie's name and the night shift hours. It wasn't much, but it was a start.

"Thanks," I said. "Mind if I leave my card? If you or Janie think of anything, give me a call."

He grunted and dropped the card next to the cash register. I headed back out.

My next stop was Rosie's Diner, a quaint little place with checkered tablecloths and the smell of fresh pie wafting from the kitchen. The lunch rush was in full swing, but I managed to snag a seat at the counter.

A harried-looking waitress with 'Doreen' on her nametag approached, coffeepot in hand. "What can I getcha, hon?"

I ordered an iced tea and a slice of pie, then pulled out the photo. "Actually, I'm hoping you might be able to help me. I'm looking for this couple. They were in town a few days ago. Any chance you've seen them? They might have been looking for jobs."

Doreen squinted as she looked at the blurry photo. A bell dinged in the back. "Sorry, I got orders. Let me think on this."

I took my time with the pie—fresh peach, homemade, and of course I'd added a scoop of vanilla ice cream—while scoping out the other customers, trying to figure out who were locals and who might just be passing through. Santa Rosa had once been a prominent stop on Route 66, a place with bustling restaurants and curio shops. But once the interstate came through, apparently the economy had settled down to what I was seeing now. I pegged two tables with working men as locals, for sure, two other tables with families that were most likely tourists.

When the two men, with Romero Construction patches on their shirts, got up to leave I interrupted and showed them the photo of my quarry. Both men shook their heads. I thanked them, figuring it had been worth a shot even though somewhat unlikely. I got much the same result from the occupants of the other table, men who obviously belonged to the Tri-Spark Electric vehicle in the parking lot. This time I remembered to hand one of them a business card. You really never knew what leads might pan out.

Doreen was making the rounds, asking if anyone needed drink refills, and she stopped beside me. "Been thinking. I do remember those kids. Cute, but a little the worse for wear. Came in here two, maybe three days ago. Ordered the cheapest things on the menu and nursed their iced teas for hours. Sometimes the boss frowns on that—people hanging around just 'cause of the AC. But I felt for 'em."

My heart raced. This was the first solid lead I'd had all day. "Did you happen to overhear any of their conversation? Or notice anything unusual?"

Doreen thought for a moment, absently refilling my iced tea. "Now that you mention it, they were arguing about something. Kept their voices low, but I could tell it was heated. The girl—red hair, right?—she seemed real upset about something. At one point she said they needed to 'come clean'."

I tried not to appear too excited. "Come clean about what?"

Doreen shrugged. "No idea. But the boy shut her down pretty quick. Said it was too dangerous, that they were in too deep."

This could be gold. "Anything else you can remember? Did they call each other by name? Any hint of where they might have been headed?"

"Sorry, hon. That's all I got. But I hope you find them. They seemed like good kids, just in a tough spot."

I thanked Doreen, left her a generous tip, and headed back out, my mind buzzing with this new information. What did they need to come clean about? What was their connection to the drug powder and bloodstain the police had found?

My next stop was the local dollar store. If the couple had been living out of their van, they might have stopped here for supplies.

The store was empty except for a bored-looking teenager restocking shelves. His nametag read 'Tyler'.

"Excuse me," I said, approaching him. "I'm looking for information on this couple. They were in town a few days ago. Any chance you've seen them?"

Tyler barely glanced at the photo. "Nah, don't think so. We get lots of people through here, y'know?"

I was about to thank him and leave when something made me pause. Tyler's disinterest seemed a little too forced. "Are you sure? Take another look. It's important."

Tyler shifted uncomfortably, not meeting my eyes. "Look, lady, I told you I haven't seen them. Now, if you'll excuse me, I've got work to do."

"Tyler," I said softly, "I think you're lying to me. And I think you know exactly who these people are."

His shoulders slumped in defeat. "Please," he whispered, "I can't talk here. Meet me out back in ten minutes."

Heart pounding, I nodded and left the store. What had I stumbled into?

Ten minutes later, I was standing in the receiving area behind the dollar store, every sense on high alert. Tyler emerged, looking nervously over his shoulder.

"Okay," he said, his voice shaky. "What do you want to know?"

"Everything," I replied. "Start with how you know them."

Tyler took a deep breath. "The guy, Rory, he's a friend of my cousin. He and Chelsea—that's his girlfriend—they showed up here a few days ago, totally freaked out."

"Last names?"

He shrugged. Kids never think to get details.

"Go on."

He scuffed one sneaker in the dirt. "Said they were in trouble, needed a place to stay."

"What kind of trouble?"

Tyler shook his head. "They wouldn't say exactly.

Something about a stolen van, some creepy guy, drugs. I didn't want to know the details. I let them crash on the couch at my house for a night, but then my mom came home early from her trip and I had to kick them out."

"Any idea where they went after that?"

"They talked about heading to Colorado. Something about a cabin up there. But I don't know if that's where they actually went, and I have no idea how to find the place anyway."

I mentally filed all this, my mind racing. It might not be much, but it was more than I'd gotten anywhere else. "Tyler, this is really important. Did they mention anyone named John Flick or Benjamin Estevez?"

Tyler's brow furrowed. "Estevez sounds kinda familiar. They whispered a lot, and seemed really freaked out about something."

Bingo. "Last question. Do you have any way to contact them?"

He hesitated, then pulled out his phone. "I've got my cousin's number. But how's that going to help?"

"Give him a call. Please? Just see if he's seen or heard from Rory within the last couple weeks."

Tyler gave a nervous glance over his shoulder, signaling he'd been away from his job too long.

"Or give me his number."

He tapped the number himself, waited until it connected. But the answer wasn't what I'd held my breath for. The cousin said he hadn't heard from Rory in two years. They hung up before I could formulate any other questions, and Tyler disappeared through the back door of the store with nothing more than a shrug toward me.

Frustrated and pumped up, in equal measure, I walked

back to my Jeep and backed out of the parking lot. I knew the couple had spent one night under a safe roof while here in town, but had they gone back to the van afterward? And now, at least I had first names. I needed to check in with Ron and see if those names matched anyone in his missing-person searches.

I wheeled into the parking lot of a row of small businesses, pulling to the side, and phoned my brother. It didn't take long to determine that he hadn't come across these two particular first names, but he thanked me for the information.

"Are you coming home tonight, or staying there?" he asked.

"I'm debating that question right now. I feel like there has to be more to learn here, plus I want to talk with the local cops again. No point in driving to Albuquerque if it means I'll need to turn around and come back."

"So … staying?"

"Yeah. I guess I'd better get a room, if you don't mind checking in on Gram and Freckles. Right now I'm trying to think of other places where a desperate couple might have eaten or shopped or otherwise shown their faces. It probably wouldn't hurt to pop in at a few more restaurants."

"Fast food places," he suggested, "where there's a dollar menu or something like that."

"Ha. You haven't been to Santa Rosa, have you? There are no chain eateries here. But you're right. I'll keep to the lower-cost options."

I was setting my phone in the Jeep's cup holder when I looked up and saw the answer staring me in the face. An auto parts store.

These kids had been driving a stolen van and it broke

down. It made sense they might try to repair it themselves—providing either of them had any mechanical know-how—rather than call a mechanic or take it to a garage where someone would likely note the VIN and might put the story together.

I locked my car and walked inside. It was a small place, compared to similar businesses in the city, but seemed fairly well stocked with a decent selection of oil, additives, belts, hoses, batteries, wiper blades, and accessories. The man behind the counter was ringing up a sale for an elderly man and offered to carry the heavy battery out for him.

Waiting, I was tempted to snoop at the old-school paper receipt book on the counter, but decided I'd best just wait my turn.

"Now—how can I help you?" the clerk (whose name was Bob, according to the patch on his shirt) asked.

I quickly explained my mission and showed him the Polaroid. "All we know is that their vehicle broke down when they reached town. I'm thinking they might have come here looking for a solution."

Bob nodded. "Yep, yeah, they did. I remember the kid's tattoos. He described what sounded like a fuel pump problem, and I looked it up in the book. We didn't have it in stock but I told him if he'd put down a deposit, I could get it ordered in from Albuquerque and have it within two days."

"Did he do that?"

"Hesitated. He was hoping he could get it sooner. And then we got into the discussion of what tools he'd need for the job. He had nothing with him. I offered to have our shop guy take a look, tow the vehicle in if they wanted us to do the work. That kind of spooked him."

I nodded, not surprised.

"The part wasn't all that expensive, about fifty bucks for a rebuilt one, and I told him I'd need a deposit of a hundred dollars for the tools he wanted to borrow. As long as he returned them in good shape, he'd get the deposit back."

"That was nice of you. But I'm guessing he didn't go for that either. Didn't have enough money?"

"Actually, he did ... Pulled out three one-hundred-dollar bills from his pocket. But the whole conversation didn't set well with the girlfriend. She dragged him over to the corner and they argued, something about 'we can't use that money' or 'it might be traced'... I don't know exactly 'cause I was technically ignoring them. But the bottom line was that she stomped out, he kind of apologized for taking my time, and they walked off. I never saw 'em again."

I thanked him for his time and headed back toward the western end of town, my head spinning with all the new information. Rory and Chelsea had plenty of cash, it seemed, and yet they had to sleep in the back of a van that must have felt like an oven, or crash on a friend's sofa. They didn't want to pay a mechanic to get the van running ... but that was probably understandable. So where had the money come from? And were the drug traces and blood on Benjamin Estevez's license the main reason why had they decided to skip town? Or had the someone Tyler had alluded to, the creepy guy, finally caught up?

I stopped at a motel I'd seen earlier, registered, and received my plastic keycard. I hadn't planned on staying the night in town, but since I would need to go out again for some dinner, I could buzz by the dollar store again and grab a toothbrush and anything else deemed essential. I was thinking chocolate chip cookies.

As I turned the AC unit up full blast and collapsed onto the bed, I pulled out my phone to call Ron and update him on the latest.

I waited until the sun was lower in the sky before I ventured out again. I came back, just before dark, with a chicken dinner in a box, assorted toiletries, chocolate chip cookies (and, okay, a few other goodies to keep me company), and a firm *no* from Janie, the evening clerk at the gas station. She hadn't seen the couple shown in the Polaroid.

One thing was clear: this case was far more complex than a simple stolen van. And somewhere out there, Rory and Chelsea were in the middle of it all. I just hoped we could find them before things turned ugly for them.

Chapter 13

The Santa Rosa police station looked exactly the same as it had two days ago, but this time, walking through those doors felt different. I'd spent the previous day chasing leads, piecing together fragments of a puzzle that was growing more complex by the hour. Now, I hoped the local law enforcement might have made progress and could supply some missing pieces for me.

Officer Martinez, the desk sergeant I'd met on my first visit, greeted me with a nod of recognition. "Back so soon, Ms. Parker?"

I managed a tired smile. "Still haven't found the answers. Is Detective Garcia in?"

Martinez shook his head. "He's out on a call. But Sergeant Peterson might be able to help you. He's been on the force longer than most of us have been alive."

He made a quick call, apparently got the okay. With a nod toward a hallway, he led me to a small office where a man who looked old enough to have ridden with Wyatt Earp sat behind a desk covered in case files. Sergeant Peterson peered at me over reading glasses that had gone out of style sometime in the early '80s.

"What can I do for you, young lady?" His voice was gruff but not unkind.

I introduced myself and gave him a quick rundown of my investigation. As I spoke, I noticed a change in his demeanor. The initial skepticism in his eyes gave way to something else— concern, maybe even a hint of trepidation.

When I finished, Peterson leaned back in his chair, the ancient wood creaking ominously. "Ms. Parker, I'm going to tell you something, and I need you to listen carefully. This case of yours is about to get a lot bigger than a missing van and a couple of runaway kids."

My heart rate picked up. "What do you mean?"

He sighed, suddenly looking every one of his many years. "Word came down from the state police office this morning. They traced the ownership of the van we impounded, ran full forensics on it, and ... the DEA is about to get involved. They've been building a case against Flick Helicopters, for months now."

The bottom dropped out of my stomach. "The DEA? You're saying Flick is involved in drug trafficking?"

Peterson nodded grimly. "It looks that way. Fentanyl, mostly. They think he's been using his helicopter business as a cover, running drugs in from Mexico and distributing them across the southwest. But they've been having trouble nailing him down. Until now."

"His mechanic was running the drugs to different cities?" I breathed, the pieces starting to click into place.

"We're not quite sure about that. But there's more. Texas police found a body yesterday, in Dallas. It's been identified as Benjamin Estevez."

I closed my eyes, a wave of sadness washing over me. I'd hoped we might find Estevez alive, that there might be an innocent explanation for all of this. "Murdered?"

"Looks that way. Throat slashed. They're still processing the scene, but early reports suggest it's connected to your case."

"The murder scene ... so he wasn't killed in the van?"

"Santa Fe didn't find that much blood in the van, not what you'd expect from a wound like this. But the scene in Texas, where the body was found, yeah. It looks like an alley in the warehouse district of Dallas is where it happened."

My mind was reeling. Flick, drug trafficking, murder— this had escalated far beyond anything I'd imagined when we took the case. And somewhere in the middle of it all were Rory and Chelsea, the two kids who'd somehow become involved in something far bigger and more dangerous than they could have ever anticipated. Check that—I really didn't know. Maybe they'd been in on the heist of the van. From their movements and descriptions, I'd assumed they were not cold-blooded killers. Now I wasn't so sure.

"What happens now?" I asked, my voice sounding small even to my own ears.

Peterson shrugged. "Drug Enforcement moves in, I suppose. I talked with Oliver Gant at the Albuquerque field office. They're coordinating with offices in Texas and along the gulf coast, and they'll share their results with

State Police here. Setting up surveillance on the operation. They'll want to question Flick, search his properties, but they'll need to have all their ducks in a row first. It's out of our hands now."

I nodded, standing up on shaky legs. "Thank you, Sergeant. You've been incredibly helpful."

As I turned toward the door, my mind was a whirlwind of conflicting thoughts and emotions. Part of me wanted to call Flick immediately, to warn him what was coming. He had been Drake's friend once, after all.

"Don't even think it," Peterson said, reading my thoughts as he walked me out. "Oh, hell, it probably doesn't matter. DEA have eyes on him. They'll know if he tries something desperate."

Another part of me, the part that had seen too many lives ruined by drugs, wanted to let Flick get caught, to experience the full force of the law.

The drive back to Albuquerque was a blur of desert landscape and turbulent thoughts. About halfway home, I couldn't take it anymore. I pulled over at a rest stop and called Drake, expecting to leave a message on his voicemail.

He picked up on the second ring. "Charlie? Everything okay?"

"Not really. Strange developments with John Flick. But I don't want to interrupt your flight. You don't need this."

"We're refueling. I've got ten minutes that are all yours."

I took a deep breath and poured out everything I'd learned. Drake listened in silence, only speaking when I'd finished.

"Jesus," he breathed. "John's involved in all that? I can't believe it."

"I know," I said softly. "Drake, what do we do? Do we

warn him?"

There was a long pause. "No," Drake said finally, his voice heavy with resignation. "No, if he's really involved in all this, he made his choice. We can't protect him from the consequences."

I nodded, even though he couldn't see me. "You're right. But … I think we need to talk to him one more time. See if he'll come clean, maybe even turn himself in. He might be able to make a deal, help take down the bigger players."

"Okay," Drake agreed. "Look, I've gotta go now. But be careful, Charlie. If even half of what you've learned is true, John could very well be a dangerous man now. You can't let him know he's going to be arrested."

I agreed. I phoned Ron and outlined a plan. My mind whirled as I drove the rest of the way to Albuquerque.

It was late afternoon when I pulled into the parking area at our office. Ron was waiting. We set up the video call in my office, both of us tense as we waited for Flick to answer.

When his face appeared on the screen, I was struck by how normal he looked. How could a man involved in drug trafficking and possibly murder look so … ordinary?

"Charlie, Ron! To what do I owe the pleasure?" His smile was as charming as ever, but now I could see the tension around his eyes, the slight twitch in his left cheek.

"John," I said, keeping my voice neutral, "we need to talk about Benjamin Estevez."

The change was subtle but unmistakable. The light in Flick's eyes dimmed, his smile becoming slightly fixed. "What about him? Have you found him?"

I took a deep breath. "John, the police found Ben's

body in the warehouse district of Dallas yesterday. He was murdered. Haven't they notified you?"

Flick's reaction was a masterclass in controlled shock. His eyes widened, his mouth dropping open in what looked like genuine surprise. But there was something off about it, like an actor who'd rehearsed the scene too many times.

"My God," he breathed. "That's … that's terrible. Poor Ben. Do they know who did it?"

I shared a glance with Ron before continuing. "They're still investigating. John, I need to ask you something, and I need you to be honest with me. What's really going on with your business? You've had a sudden influx of cash, your van was found with traces of fentanyl … John, are you involved in drug trafficking?"

Flick's face hardened, all pretense of shock vanishing. "That's a very serious accusation, Charlie. I hope you have proof to back it up."

"Come on, John," Ron cut in, his voice tinged with disappointment. "You've known Drake a long time. Just tell us the truth. Maybe we can help."

For a moment, I thought Flick might actually confess. A flicker of something—regret? fear? —passed across his face. But then the mask slipped back into place.

"The truth is, I've been very fortunate in business lately. Some new partners have invested heavily in the company. As for the van and the drugs, I have no idea how that happened. Maybe Ben was involved in something, I don't know. But I assure you, I'm running a legitimate business."

I leaned forward, locking eyes with him through the screen. "John, *if* you're using the offshore drilling rigs as handoff points for drug shipments, and *if* you feel trapped in something you can't control anymore, it's not too late.

You can still come clean, maybe even make a deal with the authorities."

Flick's laugh was cold and humorless. "You've got quite an imagination, Charlie. But let me be clear: there's nothing to come clean about. And even if there was, do you really think I'd get caught? I appreciate your concern, but I think this conversation is over."

The screen went black as he ended the call. Ron and I sat in stunned silence for a moment.

"He's in deep," Ron said finally. "Deeper than we ever imagined."

I nodded, a knot of dread forming in my stomach. "And he has no intention of getting out. So, what do we do now?"

Ron ran his hands down the sides of his face. "We do our job. We find those kids before they end up like Ben. And we let the DEA handle Flick."

I was glad to hear that Ron's opinion about the young couple mirrored my own. I'd told him about my interview with Violet Merkle and her observations. These didn't seem like savvy drug pushers, much less hardened criminals. But I've been known to misread situations in the past. I shook off that feeling, gathered my things, and headed home.

Gram must have seen me pull into the driveway. The minute my Jeep came to a stop, Freckles came bounding out her front door with Elsa right behind. I held up a hand, calling out for Gram to stop.

"It's okay, I've got her. Do *not* run down the steps." With my purse strap over one shoulder, computer bag in hand, I patted Freckles on the head and together we walked back to Elsa's.

"How's Drake doing at the fire?" she asked. One could

not fault this senior for memory problems.

I filled her in on what little I knew.

"I picked onions, peppers, and some broccoli from the garden today," she informed me. "How about a nice stir-fry for dinner?"

My expression must have conveyed surprise. Normally, Gram was more into roast beef and mashed potatoes.

"Dottie taught me how to make it. Who knew it was so simple?"

"Okay, then." I'd hoped for a shower and to change into lighter-weight clothing for the evening, but apparently everything was ready to put on the table. Even Freckles had already eaten her own dinner.

We settled at Gram's kitchen table after filling our plates, and I felt the day's tiredness seep out of me as I ate the freshest food I'd had all week. She filled me in on a conversation she'd had with Dottie this afternoon.

"Her daughter is doing fine, but I guess she's pretty impatient to get out of bed." Gram stabbed a piece of broccoli. "I know I would be—can you imagine? And she's still got three months to go."

Bedridden for three months ... no, I couldn't imagine.

"Dottie's on the warpath about her son-in-law, says he needs to get his *you-know-what* back home *now*."

"I wonder what the fight was about, why he left?"

"According to Dottie, he's 'a typical male' who doesn't want to live up to his responsibilities." She pushed some rice onto her fork. "But I don't know that it's typical. Really, Elmer was the best husband I could have asked for. He took care of all the little things around the house and he took good care of me. And Drake ... honey, you got a winner with that one."

"I really do."

"I think Dottie's hanging onto a grudge because his mother got seated closer to the front at the wedding than she did."

I gave a little smile. It seemed like weak reasoning to me. But people can hang on to old hurts for a very long time.

I went back for seconds on the stir fry and conversation turned to a political scandal Elsa had heard about on the news at noon. Shortly after I cleaned my plate I caught myself yawning. I managed to gather the dishes and put everything in the dishwasher, stowing the leftovers in her fridge for her lunch tomorrow.

"One more thing," she said, pulling a round, covered container from the cupboard. When I saw it was cherry pie, I accepted a slice to take home.

"Do you need help with anything else before I go?"

Her fists went firmly to her waist. "I'm perfectly fine on my own. As I've told Dottie many times, I do not need a babysitter."

And Dottie had told me, on several occasions, about situations where Elsa truly did need help. But I was too tired to bring it up.

"I know. Just know that you can call me if there's anything …"

"You go on home. I can see you're completely pooped. I'm going to do nothing more than put on my nightgown and watch a little TV."

I really didn't need to be told twice. It probably wouldn't hurt me to check in on the newscasts, just to see if there might be anything relevant to our case. If there was, I suspected it would have more to do with Flick's offices being raided—if that was even happening yet—than with the missing young couple.

As I headed to bed that night, my mind was a whirlpool of conflicting emotions. Besides the ever-present little worries about Drake whenever he was on a fire contract, there was disappointment in Flick, uncertainty about Rory and Chelsea, and an overwhelming sense that we were racing against a clock we couldn't see.

Tomorrow, I decided as I drifted off to sleep, tomorrow we'd redouble our efforts to find those kids. If they were involved with the drugs, I could only try to scare them into turning their lives around and helping the authorities. If they were innocents—as I tended to believe—then right now, they were the only ones we might still be able to save.

Chapter 14

Chelsea stared out the dusty cabin window, anxiety running through her like an electric current. The late afternoon sun cast long shadows across the overgrown yard, reminding her of how much time had passed since she and Rory had stumbled into this mess. She let out a sigh, her breath fogging up the glass.

"Any sign of trouble?" Rory's voice came from behind her, tense and low.

She shook her head, not turning around. "Nothing. But that doesn't mean they're not out there."

The breeze whistled through a chink in the logs somewhere, stretching her taut nerves even further. Chelsea's mind raced through their limited options for the hundredth time. The stacks of cash they'd found felt more like a curse than a blessing now, burning a hole in their backpacks.

"We can't stay here forever," she murmured, finally facing Rory. His usually cheerful face was drawn with worry, dark circles under his eyes betraying their restless nights.

"I know," he replied, running a hand through his unkempt hair. "But maybe the bikers have hit the road and moved along."

"And maybe that creepy Georgie has somehow figured out which direction we went."

Chelsea's stomach churned. They'd been over this countless times, but no clear solution had presented itself. Use the money, and they drew attention to themselves, risking arrest. Abandon it, and they'd be stranded with no resources. Call their parents, and they'd never hear the end of opinions about their reckless adventure gone horribly wrong.

"Maybe …" Chelsea started, then hesitated. The thought of reaching out to her family filled her with a complicated mix of longing and dread. "Maybe we should just call home. Take our lumps."

Rory's face tightened. "And admit defeat? Have them look at us like we're stupid kids who can't handle ourselves? My dad would—"

"Aren't we, though?" Chelsea's voice cracked. "We're in way over our heads, Rory. This isn't some fun road trip anymore. We're hiding from the cops and who knows what else."

She slumped onto the worn couch, a cloud of dust rising in the sunbeam from the window. Rory paced the small room, his restless energy a stark contrast to her defeat.

"There's got to be a way out of this," he muttered, more to himself than to her. "We just need to think."

Chelsea closed her eyes, wishing she could wake up and find this had all been a bad dream. The thrill of their initial escape now felt like a distant memory, replaced by a constant, gnawing fear. Tears threatened, but she stared toward the ceiling, blinking them back.

"What if," she said slowly, an idea forming, "we found a way to anonymously turn in the money? Leave it somewhere the police would find it, with a note explaining we didn't steal it?"

Rory stopped pacing, considering. "It's risky. We'd have to be careful not to get caught in the act."

"But it might be our best shot at clearing our names," Chelsea pressed. "We could do it at night, far from here. Then we could … maybe we could go home without fear of getting arrested."

The possibility hung in the air between them, fragile but tempting. It wasn't exactly a plan, more of a wild idea at this point, but in their desperate situation, it felt like a lifeline.

"Let's sleep on it," Rory finally said. "If it still seems like our best option in the morning, we'll figure out the details."

Chelsea nodded, a tiny spark of hope kindling in her chest, even as she wondered how they would manage the distance from this isolated cabin to the nearest police station, to turn the money in.

As the light waned, casting the cabin into shadow, she allowed herself to imagine a world where this nightmare might actually end. But the nagging voice of doubt persisted, whispering that their troubles were far from over.

Chapter 15

Georgie performed the bravest act of his life when he walked into the Santa Rosa police station. He had already debated the merits of driving to Santa Fe and trying to track down the van, with its treasure trove of cash and fentanyl, but even the dumbest of the dummies could pretty well figure that the cops had been all through it.

He'd taken a seat at Rosie's Diner during the lunchtime rush and overheard two officers discussing a bunch of different cop stuff, and they made no mention of a huge haul like that. In a town this size, yeah, that would have been big excitement. So, Georgie had to assume those damn kids had cleaned out what was rightfully his.

After all, he'd taken all the risk, he'd taken the van and hidden out, and just as he was about to leave Texas and figure out the best way to convert all that good stuff to clean money in his own name, they'd messed him up. He could picture telling this whole story to his sister, and she'd slap him upside the head for being stupid enough to think he could try to pin the crime on the young couple and then waltz right back in and take over.

Okay, yeah, yeah. He knew it had been a bad move, one that had only made sense after three whiskeys that night.

"Mr. ... um, Smith?" The uniformed desk officer was looking at him as if he'd repeated the question a few times. "How can I help you?"

"Uh, yeah, sorry. I'm a little distracted." And then he poured out the story he'd concocted about his little brother, and how they'd gotten into an argument and the kid took off. "He doesn't know his way around town—we're just passing through—so I was kind of hoping he might have been picked up and brought here for safe keeping?"

The officer shook his head. "We don't have anybody like that in custody. Give me his description and a photo if you have one. I'll have the patrol officers keep an eye out."

Georgie debated. There were both good and bad sides to having the cops looking for Rory and Chelsea. Within a minute, he decided the bad outweighed the good. "That's okay. I'll just keep looking. He's probably found a video arcade or something."

He beat it out of there before the cop could ask any more specific questions. On the front steps, he paused to catch his breath. Another dumb move. Now both he and the kids were on the radar. Stupid.

He ducked around the side of the building, in case the desk officer was looking out through the glass doors. A leafy elm tree cast nice shade on the corner, and he leaned against the rock building to catch his breath and give this situation some thought.

Okay, the kids had backpacks with them and he recalled their conversation in the van had been about doing some camping along the way to Las Vegas. The packs had seemed stuffed with gear and had sleeping bags strapped on top, so what would stop them from following through? There were a lot of small lakes and campsites in this part of the state. Georgie had brought up the map on his phone.

The van was towed day before yesterday, so how far could two kids on foot have gotten? He was willing to bet they'd decided to move along, quite possibly camping out, maybe hitchhiking again once they felt safer. They'd still be heading west. Las Vegas was a big, shiny lure reeling them in.

He relaxed against the wall and pulled out his phone again, bringing up the map. He could retrieve the blue truck from where he'd left it over on Second Street (a quick congratulations to himself on not driving a stolen truck right up to the front of the cop shop). Once mobile again, he could cruise the lakes and campgrounds that were within a day's walk. After that …

His thoughts were interrupted by a female voice nearby, talking on a cell phone. He looked up to see a nice-looking thirty-something woman in slim jeans and a t-shirt that fit just right. Long, auburn hair gleamed in the sunlight, like a copper penny. But what caught his attention were her words when he overheard the names Chelsea and Rory.

Staring at his phone screen, he stepped out and started to follow her.

" … one lead that might pan out. A relative has a cabin somewhere near Trinidad." A pause. "See what you can find on that. Right. Yeah, last names would be a plus, for sure."

She dropped the phone into a side pocket of the bag that was slung over her shoulder, and Georgie peeled away. He couldn't believe his luck.

With a huge grin, he shifted his map search for any place called Trinidad and discovered a little town in Colorado, just north of the New Mexico state line. He mapped out the quickest route and was on the way.

He didn't know what vehicle those kids would be in, but he had the advantage of knowing their last names. He was thirty minutes down the road before another thing began to nag at him. Who was the woman, and why was she also looking for Rory Whittaker and Chelsea Brown?

Chapter 16

I pulled into the parking lot at the office, stifling a yawn as I cut the engine. Yesterday had been a long one and yet I'd awakened early. The early morning sun was just starting to peek over Sandia Crest, painting the sky in hues of pink and orange. Despite the beautiful dawn, my mind was clouded with worry over our missing couple. I'd tossed and turned all night, my dreams filled with images of Chelsea and Rory in various states of distress. To my surprise, Ron was already at the office.

Shaking off the remnants of sleep, I grabbed my travel mug of coffee and headed inside. My brother sat hunched over his computer with a look of intense concentration.

"Morning, Charlie," he said without looking up. "Got some stuff for you."

"You're working early. Sally isn't even here yet," I remarked, setting my bag down on my desk, then crossing the hall to his office.

"Yeah, if I'm going to finish the Borkin job and help out with this Flick case, I gotta put in some extra time. Plus, with the boys home for summer vacation, I'm not getting anything done at home."

"What've you got?"

Ron swiveled his chair to face me, a stack of papers in his hand. "From the missing persons reports I got last names for the kids. Chelsea Brown and Rory Whittaker. She's twenty-one, he's twenty-two. Both from San Diego, both sets of parents filed reports after the pair of them left in anger and haven't been reachable for more than a month. I've been cross-referencing descriptions matching Chelsea and Rory across several states."

I felt a surge of anticipation. "Any hits?"

"Maybe," Ron said, handing me the papers. "There's one that caught my eye. A couple matching their description was spotted at a biker bar a little south of Starkville, Colorado, a day or so ago. Seems there was a little altercation when some of the bikers came on a little too strong. The bar owner didn't like having some chairs smashed up and a window broken, and he called the cops."

I scanned the report, my heart rate picking up. "Starkville is just south of Trinidad, and that's where my interviewee said something about a family cabin. This could be them. Good work, Ron."

He nodded, a hint of a smile on his face. "Thought you'd want to check it out ASAP."

"You thought right," I said, already reaching for my car keys. "I'm heading to Trinidad now. Keep digging, will you? See if you can find any more background on these kids—

where they might have been headed, their family situation, that sort of thing. Sounds like things must have been tense at home if the parents admitted they left in anger."

"On it," Ron replied, turning back to his computer.

"Oh. And … if I'm not back by closing time, can you take Freckles home with you and also check in on Gram to be sure she doesn't need anything?"

He gave me a blank look.

"Ron … surely, I told you … Dottie was called out of town and Gram's on her own. I've been in regular contact, but you know—"

"She's over ninety and—" He interrupted himself by waving me off. "Consider it done."

I drove to the nearest station to fill up for the trip, patting my Jeep on the door as the pump ticked through the numerals. "We're getting a lot of miles under our belts this week, aren't we?"

The drive north took a little over three hours, giving me plenty of time to mull over the latest news on the case. I didn't picture two young people from California just accidentally stumbling upon a van from south Texas. We already had our suspicions about the shady things John Flick's business was into—had the couple somehow known about the drugs or the cash?

Maybe they saw an opportunity that looked like easy pickings? But to hijack the van and kill the driver … That sounded way more hardened-criminal than I'd imagined this pair. I had Violet Merkle's impressions in my head, that they were kids who were broke and down on their luck.

We needed to learn more, between Ron's deeper background checks and whatever I might learn here in Colorado. I exited, following my GPS locator for this biker bar Ron had told me about.

I shook off the uneasy feeling that crept down my spine when I saw it was a run-down joint called The Rusty Nail. The wooden siding was in need of fresh paint, and the metal roofing sported warped and dented places. I had to wonder if the owner's filing a damage report for a broken window was a way to get his insurance company to provide enough for other repairs as well.

The parking lot was mostly empty, save for a few beat-up trucks and a line of motorcycles gleaming in the midday sun. Twangy, country music drifted out.

Taking a deep breath, I pulled open the screen door and stepped inside. The bar was dimly lit, the air thick with the smell of stale beer and cigarette smoke. A few patrons looked up as I entered, their eyes curious, not especially friendly.

I approached the bar, where a burly man with a thick beard was wiping down glasses. "What can I get you?" he grunted.

"Information, if you've got it," I replied, sliding onto a barstool. I pulled out a photo of Chelsea and Rory that Ron had copied from the missing persons reports, far better images than the blurry one Violet had snapped. "I'm looking for these two. They might have been in here a couple days ago."

The bartender barely glanced at the photo, grunted, and didn't say anything.

I wasn't deterred. "Look, I'm not here to cause trouble. The owner of this place reported there was a little dustup of some kind, and we thought this couple might have been involved. I'm just trying to make sure these kids are safe. Their families are worried sick."

His expression softened slightly, but he shook his head. "Sorry, lady. I heard about it but I wasn't on duty that night. You can ask around. Some of these folks are regulars, but if it involved bikers they may have just been passing through."

I tried a few more patrons, but got similar responses. Either they genuinely didn't remember Chelsea and Rory, or they were closing ranks to protect them. Either way, I was getting nowhere fast.

Feeling discouraged, I headed back to my Jeep. As I was about to get in, I noticed a woman watching me from a doorway at the back corner of the building. She was probably in her late fifties, with dark hair that was growing out gray, and she wore a stained, white apron. She looked nervous, glancing around as if to make sure no one was watching.

I approached her slowly, putting on a smile. "Hi there. I'm Charlie. You work here?"

She nodded but didn't relax much.

"I'm looking for some information about a couple of kids who might have been here recently. Someone said there was an incident with some bikers. I'm just trying to find out where the young couple went afterward."

She stepped out from what must have been a storage area behind the kitchen, hesitating. "I heard you talking to Butch, but I'm not sure if I ..."

"Please," I said softly, holding out the photos. "These kids could be in trouble. I just want to help them."

After a moment, she nodded. "They were here," she whispered. "The girl—she seemed scared. They were trying to sell something, I think. I don't know—that's just an impression I got when I carried someone's order out to a table. But then some of the guys started getting interested, and these kids ... they took off real quick."

"Do you know where they went?" I asked, trying to keep the urgency out of my voice.

She shook her head. "Just ran out the front door and took off running into the woods."

I remembered my conversation with the guy at the dollar store in Santa Rosa. "Are there any cabins around here? Vacation places or rentals?"

She bit her lip for a moment, thinking. "I'm not sure ... I live in Trinidad so I'm not real familiar with this area ... But I think if you drive a couple miles on up to Starkville and get off the interstate there, it seems there are some little dirt roads that go back into the forest. I suppose there could be cabins up in there."

"Thank you so much ..." But she didn't take the bait and provide her name. I barely got one of my business cards pressed into her hand before she ducked back inside.

As I backed out of The Rusty Nail parking lot, my mind was racing. Chelsea and Rory had been here, all right. But where had they gone? And what were they trying to sell? My thoughts immediately leapt to the traces of fentanyl found in the van. If they'd taken the drugs from the van and were now pushing them, it would change my ideas about their innocence in this whole mess.

Following instructions from my nameless informant at the bar, I made my way back to I-25 and exited at Starkville. The little roadside spot had a surprising number of dwellings on side roads, plus a solid two-star hotel and an eatery. I roamed in the general direction I'd been given and came to a county road that seemed promising as it led into a more heavily wooded area.

The dirt road became a two-lane track. Driveways branched off it and I could see rustic cabins. None of the driveways had recent tire prints, so I kept going. A couple miles in, I spotted a cabin on the right and another on the left with evidence that vehicles had come and gone. But the key was, they were gone now. Both places had curtains drawn at the windows. A single set of tracks had approached and left again, and I became discouraged that it was probably someone like myself who was wandering without knowing where they were going.

Powering my window down I sniffed the air for any hint of woodsmoke. None. But then again, the weather had been warm all week. Who would light a fireplace? I debated whether to keep going, not knowing how long this road continued and not feeling a lot of hope. After all, the idea that Chelsea and Rory would be staying at a relative's cabin had come from more of a rumor than an actual fact. Still, the woman back at The Rusty Nail had identified the pair. I couldn't completely give up.

I pressed on until the dirt road narrowed even more, and I spotted a pickup truck coming toward me. I pulled as far to the side as I could get, and it edged forward. When the driver came alongside, I waved for him to stop.

"Hey, I think I may be a little lost," I said, concocting a story on the spot. "Some friends are staying at a cabin up here somewhere but they didn't give very good directions."

The gray-haired man with an impressive mustache grinned and nodded. "Yep, I hear that a lot."

"It's a young couple and the cabin belongs to his uncle. I think the last name is Whittaker. Do you know the place?"

He shook his head slowly back and forth. "That name ain't familiar. And I been here more than forty years."

I bit my lip, giving him another moment to think. "What about a place with people coming and going recently? I think they got here two or three days ago."

"Couple of these places had weekenders up, but I think they all left. I'd say if you see a vehicle out front it might be worth stopping to ask. What're they drivin'?"

"That's the problem. I don't really know."

He nibbled at the mustache for a few seconds. "I spotted a white SUV down by the highway, had New Mexico tags, and there was a sticker on the window, you know, the kind the cops put. Like a 'move it or lose it' notice. If they was drivin' that, they mighta walked on in to the cabin. It's a couple miles, but you said they're young. They could handle it."

I nodded. "Is the SUV still there today?"

"Didn't notice." He glanced down the road behind me, clearly ready to get on with his day.

"Thanks. Hopefully I can find them."

He drove on downhill and I proceeded up the road, wondering what I was doing here. The mission was beginning to look hopeless. As I reached the end of the road, only one log house appeared occupied, most likely by the guy I'd just spoken to. An older model Suburban sat in the driveway. Two dogs went into a barking frenzy, leaping and warning me away, but they didn't leave their yard. A woman stepped out onto the porch, calling to them, giving me a wave. I used the wide spot at the end of the road to turn around.

Making my way slowly downhill again, I paused at each place where a driveway branched off. I got out of the Jeep each time, studying the ground. Two of the cabins showed tire tracks leading in and out, but the dwellings themselves were closed up tight—most likely places used by the weekenders the man had described. A third place had faint tracks that dated back to the last storm; they were definitely older than a few days.

I tried to figure out Chelsea and Rory's moves. They'd abandoned the yellow van and then come all the way from Santa Rosa in some kind of vehicle. Yet it seemed they had come and gone from The Rusty Nail on foot. Maybe Ron could run a trace on that SUV down by the highway and find out if it had been stolen in Santa Rosa. I pulled out my phone to make a call, but this far from town and down in the trees, I couldn't get a signal.

Another hour ticked by as I kept checking driveways, with no luck at all. I wound my way back to the cheap motel I'd passed, thinking maybe the kids had stopped there instead. The desk clerk didn't remember them, and although my RJP Investigations business card got the guy to check their records, no matches turned up.

A large metal building across the parking lot housed a tire shop and garage, so I walked over there. Sitting at the southern edge of the property was the SUV I'd heard about. New Mexico plates, an older model vehicle that could probably be hotwired to start it. Both the front seats and the back were empty but I took pictures anyway.

When I walked into the tire shop, a guy in dungarees looked up.

"That white SUV out there … did you see who left it?"

"Nope. Sat there two days and then I called the cops. It ain't mine and it's taking up valuable space on my lot."

I glanced out the front windows, noting that the lot was ninety-nine percent empty.

"Would have thought they'd towed it by now, but there

it sets." He turned back to a calculator with a grimy keypad where he'd been punching numbers.

I offered a weak-sounding thanks and left. Now what? I had to believe Chelsea and Rory were somewhere in the area but every lead so far had become a dead end.

I looked at the depressing little motel across the way and decided I couldn't face a night there. Although it was getting late in the day and I was dead tired, I headed the Jeep toward home.

Chapter 17

When I woke up the next morning, I congratulated myself on making the right decision. A solid night's sleep had done wonders. Not to mention getting the chance to check in on Elsa and receiving plenty of doggie kisses from Freckles.

Back at the office, I found Ron still hard at work. He looked up as I peeked through his doorway, his expression eager. "Any luck?"

I gave him the description and plate number of the SUV in Starkville, then filled him in on what I'd learned at the bar. "It's not much," I concluded, "but at least we know we're on the right track."

Ron nodded, then gestured to his computer screen. "I've got some background info on our runaways—if we're calling them that. Turns out they're both originally from San Diego and are legally adults."

"San Diego?" I echoed, surprised. "That's quite a way from here. What else did you find?"

"Well, I managed to track down contact information for Chelsea's parents and her best friend," Ron said, handing me a notepad with phone numbers. "Thought you might want to give them a call, see what light they can shed on the situation."

I nodded, taking the page. "Good thinking. I'll start with the parents."

I walked across the hall to my own office, dropped my laptop bag on my chair, and set my coffee mug on the desk. While my computer booted up, I opened the blinds on my windows to let in more light. Freckles managed to talk me out of a cookie from the tin I keep on the bookshelf, before I made it back to my chair, picked up the phone, and dialed the first number on my list.

The phone rang several times before a woman's voice answered, sounding tired and strained.

"Mrs. Brown? This is Charlie Parker from RJP Investigations in Albuquerque."

"Yes …?" Wary.

"I'm calling about your daughter, Chelsea."

There was a sharp intake of breath on the other end of the line. "Have you found her? Is she okay?"

The raw concern in her voice caught me off guard. This didn't sound anything like the uncaring parents Chelsea had described to Tyler in Santa Rosa.

"We're still looking for her, Mrs. Brown," I said gently. "But we've had some good leads. I'm trying to piece together why she might have been in Texas and New Mexico recently."

"What? Oh my gosh." Her breath whooshed out, as if she'd just plopped down onto a soft couch. "Texas? I had no idea. She doesn't know anyone there."

"We're not sure either. Our client had a van that went missing. We began by trying to track that. It seems your daughter and her boyfriend somehow got involved."

"She and that *guy* are traveling the country in a *van*?"

"Well, not now. The police have the van. I guess I've kind of taken up the mission of finding Chelsea and Rory because I had a feeling they might be in trouble."

"Oh, Lord. Chelsea has always been a good kid—smart, driven, eager to go to college. But this past year, things changed. She started hanging out with a new crowd," Mrs. Brown explained, her voice thick with emotion. "Staying out late, sneaking around. We tried to talk to her, but she just shut us out. There was a blowup between us. And the next day, she was just ... gone. Took her backpack and a few of her favorite books ... and not much else. I've called her phone and sent texts nearly every day. She never responds."

I jotted down notes as she spoke, my brow furrowing. This was starting to paint a very different picture of our missing couple. This didn't sound like an uncaring or abusive parent. "And what about Rory?" I asked. "Did you know him?"

"Not well," Mrs. Brown replied. "Chelsea had only known him for a few months. Her dad and I thought he might be a bad influence, but she wouldn't listen to a word we said on *that* subject. Now I wish ..." She trailed off, and I could hear the regret in her voice.

After reassuring Mrs. Brown that we were doing everything we could to find Chelsea and bring her home safely, I ended the call. My mind was whirling with this new information as I filled in my notes.

I was about to pick up the phone for the next call on my list when my cell pinged with a text.

Sorry I bailed on lunch the other day. How about today?

I'd forgotten all about seeing Linda Casper this week and it made me feel rotten. I tapped the message and sent a quick reply: **Absolutely. When? Where?**

Is early ok? Got a full office of patients this afternoon.

And that's how I ended up setting aside my phone call list and making the drive up to the northeast heights to meet Linda at Monroe's on Osuna. I spotted her snappy little red Tesla in the lot when I arrived. She had already gotten us a table at the far side of the room. With its Saltillo tile floors and hard surfaces, the place could get pretty noisy when it filled up—as it did every day. I walked over and gave her a hug.

"How's your dad doing?"

She shook her head, her blonde curls swaying. "Not good. He's in hospice now and I've had to get him into a facility since there's no one at home to be his caregiver. It's hard."

"I'm so sorry."

She took a deep breath as she scanned the menu. "I'm doing lots of meditation and yoga to get myself through it." Her blue eyes focused on my face intently. "You look a little stressed, yourself. Yoga would be good for you too."

"Um ..." I remembered the last time she'd talked me into taking yoga classes, with the uptight instructor I'd wanted to kill. Rita. I didn't—I swear—and we caught the real killer. But it had kind of put me off traveling that path.

Linda apparently read my thoughts. "Look, we have a

yoga instructor who comes into my office each morning and afternoon. She's wonderful. Gives classes for all my patients who want to come. And she's nothing like that Rita person. Ever since I studied more about Eastern medicine, I've expanded my facilities to include a lot of helpful practices, in addition to the traditional stuff I was taught in med school."

I said I'd think about it, and fortunately our server arrived just in time to save me from making a commitment. I ordered a beef burrito and Linda got a big salad. Okay, so maybe there was a healthier lifestyle waiting for me out there.

We spent the next forty-five minutes catching up. She asked about Drake and how things were going at RJP. I had to admit the former was wonderful and it was the latter that was stressing me out right now. When I said something about how much time I'd spent on the road in the past week, she glanced at her watch.

"Oh no, I'd better get going," she said, reaching for her purse. "I'm so sorry I can't linger and talk all afternoon."

"I get it. Solidly booked." I waved off her money. "I'll get it this time, which means we have to do this again, and it'll be your treat then."

She sent me a grateful smile before turning toward the exit. I took a few more minutes to polish off my sopapilla, wipe the honey from my fingers, and stop at the front counter to pay our bill. I'd missed my good friend and made a promise to myself that I would be better about keeping in touch.

Back in my Jeep, I hit the freeway toward the valley again, already thinking about my next steps in tracking the missing young couple. It was time to get a different perspective.

At my desk, Ron had left a note saying the data I'd given him on the white SUV abandoned in Starkville matched a report from Santa Rosa. An Explorer taken from a used car lot. I stuck that aside, picked up his notation with the California numbers, and dialed Chelsea's best friend, a girl named Megan. She answered on the second ring.

I introduced myself and told her I was trying to find Chelsea and Rory, to be sure they were all right. "Do you have a few minutes to talk?"

There was a pause, then a quiet, "Okay."

"Megan, I'm trying to understand what was going on in Chelsea's life before she left. Her mother mentioned some changes in her behavior. Did you notice anything?"

Megan sighed heavily. "Yeah, I noticed. Chelsea ... she was going through a lot, you know? Her parents, they're not bad people, but they just didn't get her."

"How do you mean?" I prompted gently.

"They had all these expectations for her. Top grades, perfect behavior, the works. Her mom even had a certain college picked out for her and had sent in the applications without even asking if Chels wanted to go there. It was a religious school, and—my own opinion—not a good fit for her. Chelsea felt like she could never measure up, no matter how hard she tried. And then she met Rory…"

"What's he like?"

"Rory is a whirlwind. He's charming, adventurous, always talking about his plans to see the world. To Chelsea, he represented everything her carefully controlled life wasn't. I tried to warn her," Megan said, her voice tinged with regret.

I scribbled notes as she talked.

"Rory seemed nice enough, but there was something … I don't know, unstable about him. Like he was always chasing the next big thing. I was worried he'd get Chelsea into trouble."

"And did you share these concerns with Chelsea's parents?" I asked.

"No," Megan admitted. "I should have, maybe. But Chelsea made me promise not to. She said her parents wouldn't understand, that they'd just try to keep her and Rory apart."

"Did either of them mention any specific place they wanted to go, somewhere in Texas or maybe Colorado?"

"Las Vegas. Rory was in a band for a while, in high school. He seemed to think he could get work as a musician. So, in Texas that would be Austin. But Vegas … he just knew he'd get into a backup band for one of the big-name performers. They make decent money, and he was all about that."

"Did he have any connections, to achieve that dream?"

"Ha. He didn't even have his own guitar. Borrowed a Fender from one of the other guys in the band, even though he liked to carry it around and pretend it was his. I think finally Michael made him give it back. I guess Rory figured if he hooked up with a band in some other city that they'd just provide him an instrument."

"Have you spoken with Chelsea since they left California?" At her silence, I added. "I won't say anything to her mother."

"Two calls. About a month ago, she called me and said they were in Austin. Rory was making the rounds of the clubs and thought he had a good lead on a gig or two. They'd run through their money and she wondered if I could Venmo her a little bit to keep them going until he got paid."

"And ... did you?"

"No way. My job is only part-time and barely makes my car payment. If I didn't live at home with my parents I'd be in a mess. I mean, I told her I would if I could, but sorry."

"And you talked to her another time?"

"Yeah, gosh, I guess it was two weeks ago, or about that. I called her and felt like she just *happened* to answer. I wanted to be sure there were no hard feelings about my not sending her some money. But she kind of blew me off. Said they were fine. They had money now, lots of it. I felt really bad because her attitude was kind of ... I don't know ... like she didn't need me as a friend anymore." Megan's voice shook a little. "I've tried to call and text her a bunch of times since then and she just ignores me."

I told her that even though the two were on the run, I'd had verified sightings of them, alive and well, within recent days. "Just hang in there. I think we'll find them, and I'll be sure to tell her you really want to hear from her. She'll be okay."

As we ended the call, I really hoped that was true.

Chapter 18

Chelsea squinted against the harsh sunlight, her feet aching as she trudged along the uneven roadside. Pea-sized gravel kept popping into her shoes, and pulling it out while managing her backpack was a real pain. The remote cabin that had been their sanctuary for the past few days was now just a speck in the rearview mirror of this stupid adventure.

The white Explorer they'd hotwired and left near the tire shop in Starkville had been tagged by law enforcement. Rory had bravely (stupidly!) peeled the sticker off and started the vehicle, but she was a bundle of twitchy nerves the whole time they were in it. They used it to get a few miles up the road, but she insisted they leave it behind. She was hoping she would spot another possibility, but so far no luck with that. Meanwhile, they were back to hitching rides.

Beside her, Rory's face was set in a grim expression, his usual carefree demeanor long since evaporated. "We should've stayed at the cabin," he muttered, kicking at a pebble.

Chelsea sighed, fatigue and frustration coloring her voice. "And do what? We kind of stand out in a small community where everyone knows everyone. We've been over this, Rory. We can't hide inside a cabin forever. And we can't be driving a stolen car that's already been tagged once. Nothing's worked out the way we thought it would. I just want to get back home, try to fix things with my parents."

"And if that doesn't work out?" Rory asked, a hint of bitterness in his tone.

"Then I'll stay with Megan, get a job," Chelsea replied, her mind drifting to thoughts of her best friend. The idea of seeing a familiar face felt like a lifeline in their current chaos. "I'm just … I'm so tired of running, Rory. Aren't you?"

"I still think I can pick up some gigs in—"

She cut him short with a look. He was a three-chord player, if that. Why hadn't she seen his bullshit side before?

Rory went quiet, his silence speaking volumes.

As long as they'd stayed near the I-25 onramps, they'd gotten rides, although way too short, and being so visible was scary. That creep was still out there somewhere. South of Springer, they'd decided to try a less-busy road. Now, they walked on, the sparse traffic on the road a reminder of just how far they'd strayed from civilization. Each passing car sent a jolt of hope through Chelsea as she stuck out her thumb, only to be dashed as it sped by without slowing.

As the sun climbed higher in the sky, the weight of their situation pressed down on them like a physical force. Chelsea's mind raced with possibilities, each one seeming worse than the last. Finally, she voiced the thought that had been nagging at her for days.

"Maybe ... maybe we should just turn ourselves in," she said hesitantly.

Rory stopped in his tracks, turning to face her with wide, disbelieving eyes. "To the police? Are you crazy? After everything we've been through?"

Chelsea held her ground. "Think about it, Rory. We're probably gonna get caught anyway. If we go to the police, explain everything—"

"Explain what?" Rory cut her off, his voice rising. "That we stole a van full of drugs? That we took off with a wad of cash that isn't ours? And, oh yeah—bloodstains that we can't explain. They'll lock us up and throw away the key!"

"We didn't know what was in the van," Chelsea argued, her own temper flaring. "We didn't know about the blood or the drugs. If we just tell the truth—"

Rory laughed, a harsh, humorless sound. "The truth? And once they've locked us up, they'll never keep looking for that creepy Georgie. Wake up, Chelsea. We're screwed, no matter what we do."

Chelsea felt tears of frustration prickling at the corners of her eyes. This wasn't how it was supposed to go. Their great adventure, their escape from the suffocating expectations of her parents and the constant criticism of his—it had all gone so horribly wrong.

"Fine," she snapped, turning away from Rory. "You do what you want. I'm going home."

With that, she started walking faster, her strides long and angry. She heard Rory calling after her, but she didn't turn back. The sound of his footsteps kept a steady pace, gradually dropping back, but he left her alone.

Chelsea felt her anger gradually ebbing, giving way to a gnawing fear—of exhaustion, of spending a night out on a roadside—when she heard the rumble of an approaching vehicle. Hope surged through her as she turned, thumb outstretched.

The blue pickup truck slowed as it approached, and Chelsea felt a wave of relief wash over her. As the vehicle came to a stop beside her, she stepped forward, a grateful smile on her face.

Then she saw the driver.

Chelsea froze as she locked eyes with Georgie Lafarge, the very man who had set this whole nightmare in motion. His face, once jovial and friendly, now held a predatory gleam that sent shivers down her spine.

"Well, well," Georgie drawled, a slow smile spreading across his face. "Looks like my luck's finally turning around. Hop in, sweetheart. Let's have a little chat."

Chelsea took an instinctive step back, her heart pounding in her chest. "I … I'm fine, thanks. My friend is just up the road, we're—"

She started to run, but with a speed that belied his size, Georgie lunged out the door and caught up with her, his hand closing around her wrist in an iron grip. Chelsea screamed, the sound lost in the empty landscape as Georgie yanked her toward the truck.

Her eyes sought out Rory. He was at least a quarter mile back, shouting and running toward her now, but he would never catch up in time.

"Let go of me!" she yelled, struggling against Georgie's hold. But it was no use. With the strength of a desperate man, he pushed her into the truck, slamming the door shut behind her, and tossed her pack into the back.

"Now then," he said, his voice deceptively calm as they started to roll. "Why don't you tell me where that cash of mine got to?"

Chelsea's mind raced, fear clouding her thoughts. She glanced at the door handle, wondering if she could jump out, but Georgie hit the lock button and she heard it click, sealing her inside.

"Cash? I don't know what you're talking about," she managed to say, her voice shaking. "Please, just let me go."

Georgie's laugh was cold and humorless. "Oh, I don't think so, sweetheart. You and your boyfriend have caused me a whole lot of trouble. It's time to settle up. We're gonna stop here in a little bit and talk it all out."

Chelsea's eyes darted around, desperately seeking some means of escape. But Georgie kept a tight grip on her wrist, his eyes flicking between her and the road ahead. The truck hit a pothole and he slowed down a little.

Suddenly, a flash of movement in the side mirror caught Chelsea's attention. Rory—running full tilt behind them. Her heart fluttered. He'd been a track star in school; she knew he could run miles, but trying to catch a moving vehicle? It wouldn't take long for any passing motorist to recognize this situation as trouble.

Georgie must have noticed too. He swore under his breath, sped up for a mile or so to leave Rory behind, then abruptly turned off the two-lane road onto a narrow dirt track. The truck bounced and jolted as they sped down the uneven path, kicking up a cloud of dust behind them.

After what felt like an eternity, but was probably only a few minutes, a dilapidated structure came into view. As they drew closer, Chelsea realized it was an old barn, its weathered boards gray with age and neglect. Her danger-alarm was screaming inside her head.

Georgie brought the truck to a stop, the sudden silence after the roar of the engine almost deafening. "End of the line, sweetheart," he said, yanking Chelsea out of the truck.

She stumbled, her legs weak with fear, as Georgie marched her toward the barn. The musty smell of old hay and rotting wood assaulted her senses as they entered the shadowy interior.

"All right," Georgie said, pushing Chelsea roughly against a support post, grabbing up a length of rope and tying her in place. "Let's try this again. Where's my money?"

She stared at him for long minutes, keeping her mouth shut. He moved in and grabbed her chin, forcing her to meet his eyes, to catch a whiff of his putrid breath as he repeated the question. When she shook her head, he slapped her face.

Chelsea opened her mouth to respond, but before she could, a voice rang out from the barn entrance.

"Let her go!"

Chelsea's heart thumped as she saw Rory standing there, his chest heaving from the exertion of his run. He held a broken fence rail like a baseball bat, ready to take on her captor. But her relief quickly turned to horror as she saw the gleam in Georgie's eyes.

"Arrrrghhhh!" Georgie lunged, grabbing the fence post. Rory tried to dodge but wasn't quite fast enough. There was a scuffle, a cry of pain, as both men rolled on the dirt floor, flailing. Georgie lost patience for a tussle and slugged Rory in the gut, doubling him over. In under a minute Rory was tied to a post on the other side of the barn.

Georgie ran out of the barn and was gone a few minutes. Then, suddenly, he was back and looming over them with a look of manic frustration.

"Your damn packs are empty! I'm done playing games," he snarled, pacing between them. "One of you is going to tell me where that money is, or things are going to get real unpleasant real quick."

Chelsea met Rory's eyes across the barn, seeing her own fear reflected back at her. How had it come to this? Just days ago, they'd been two kids on an adventure, full of dreams and plans for the future. Now, they were at the mercy of a desperate criminal, miles from help, with no way out.

"We don't have it," Rory said, his voice strained but defiant. "We got rid of it. It's gone."

Georgie's face contorted with rage. He strode over to Rory, grabbing a fistful of his hair. "You're lying," he hissed. "That was my ticket out of here, and you weasels ruined everything!"

"It's the truth!" Chelsea cried out, desperate to draw Georgie's attention away from Rory. "We were scared, we didn't know what to do with it. We ... we left it behind."

Georgie released Rory, turning his furious gaze on Chelsea. For a moment, she thought he might strike her, but then something in his expression changed. A calculating look came into his eyes, sending a fresh wave of fear through her.

"Left it behind, where?" he asked, his voice dangerously soft.

Chelsea hesitated, her mind racing. Should she tell the truth? Make up a lie? What would be safest for them?

Her hesitation cost her. Georgie's hand shot out, grabbing her chin and forcing her to look at him. "Where?" he demanded again.

"The cabin!" Chelsea blurted out, tears streaming down her face. "We left it at the cabin we were staying in."

"Where?"

"It's in Colorado."

His eyes glittered dangerously. "Exactly where? Show me! Draw me a map on the floor." He yanked the shoe and sock off her right foot, pressing her big toe into the dust.

She glanced up at Rory, uncertain. He nodded.

"Now!" Georgie wasn't messing around. He twisted her ankle and scraped the toe into the dirt again.

"Okay, okay." Chelsea began to draw lines, pointing out the exit from I-25, the county road where they'd made the turn, and the driveway to the cabin. "It's got blue curtains on the front windows."

Georgie stared at her for a long moment, as if trying to gauge the truth of her words. Then, abruptly, he released her foot and strode toward the barn entrance.

"You'd better hope you're telling the truth," he said, pausing at the door. "Because if that money isn't there, things are gonna get real ugly for you two when I get back." To prove his point, he pulled something from his pocket and flicked the switchblade open.

With that, he was gone. Chelsea heard the roar of the blue truck's engine, fading as Georgie drove away. She sagged against her bonds, relief and terror warring within her.

"Chelsea?" Rory's voice was small, scared. "What are

we going to do?"

She looked at him, seeing the boy she'd thought she knew so well in a whole new light. They were both so young, so unprepared for the harsh realities they'd stumbled into.

"I don't know, Rory," she said honestly. "But we have to find a way out of here before he comes back."

As they began to struggle against their bonds, Chelsea's mind raced with possibilities. How long would it take Georgie to reach the cabin and realize the money wasn't there? How much time did they have? It would take him at least two hours to drive to the cabin and back, and however much time would he spend looking for the cash. And even if they managed to get free, where could they go?

The late afternoon sun slanted through the cracks in the barn walls, a frightening reminder of the passing time.

As she worked at the ropes binding her wrists, ignoring the pain as the rough fibers bit into her skin, Chelsea made a silent vow. If they got out of this—*when* they got out of this—she would make things right. With her parents, with the authorities, with everyone. No more running, no more lies.

But first, they had to survive.

Chapter 19

I tapped my pen on the desk after hanging up with Chelsea's friend Megan. A picture was forming of a girl who was unhappy at home, feeling rebellious because of her over-controlling parents, striking out on her own with a guy who ... what? I didn't know a whole lot about him.

So I called the number I'd gotten for the Whittaker household. A man answered.

"Mr. Whittaker?"

"Yeah?" Cautious. Ready to hang up if I was a telemarketer.

I quickly introduced myself and my purpose for the call, asking whether he'd heard from Rory in recent weeks.

"Nope. Didn't expect to neither." A voice hardened by years of smoking.

"Why is that?"

"Him and me, we didn't part on the best of terms, let's just say."

I let the silence sit there, hoping he would elaborate. And he did. This was a man who needed for someone to hear his side of the story.

"Rory blew his big chance in life. Unlike his two older brothers, he really had a shot at college. The rest of us, we're stuck working down at the Navy yards, lifers stuck in a pay grade that barely makes ends meet. Rory was a star athlete in high school. Track. Whoo, that kid could run. Beat all the school records, then the district records. Got recruited—big time." He paused, taking a breath that sounded a little ragged.

I gathered there was more.

"Then what does he do? Some long-haired, no-good at the school puts a guitar in his hands. He gets where he can strum out a few popular tunes and then he's in a band with four other no-talents, and then he's arguing with me that he can make more in the music business than running track in school. The *music business*—hah! None of them kids know shit about music and even less about business.

"But I point that out to my son and he argues that Tommy—or one of them in the band—has an uncle who has a cousin, or some such crap. He's gonna get 'em in as backup players for this big-name singer and their careers will be set. They'll have an album out in a few months' time. Says it'll take him years to get through college and years after that before he'll make any money. In Austin, they'll have work right away and everybody'll be making millions within a year."

"Seems pretty unrealistic …"

"Exactly! And that's what I told him, but he said he'd already turned down all the scholarship offers. He had full-ride offers from some good schools—turned 'em down! And that's when we really had words. I basically told 'im to get out. Good luck with this stupid dream of theirs, and don't come crawling back to me when it doesn't work out."

Whittaker stopped for a long, raspy cough before he spoke again. "So, I'm guessing the reason for your call is because the little s.o.b.'s in trouble somewhere."

Was I going to add fuel to his fire by telling him the whole story? This didn't seem like the right time for that. I hedged by saying, "I'm mainly trying to track down his girlfriend, Chelsea Brown. I've spoken with her mother and a friend, and they're worried because they haven't heard anything either."

"Yeah, that girl. There's always a girl behind every stupid decision a high school kid makes, isn't there?"

I really had to bite my tongue at that statement.

"Well, she's the one introduced him to a couple of those turds in the band, so I got no use for her whatsoever. I wish you luck." And with that he hung up.

Okay. I slowly replaced the receiver on its cradle. I was trying to decide my next move when the intercom buzzed me. Sally told me it was the detective from the Santa Rosa police department.

"Detective Garcia."

"Hi, Charlie," he said. "Got a minute?"

"Of course. What's up?"

"You asked me to let you know if we got any updates on that couple we talked about — the ones with the stolen van? So yeah, we got a report this morning. They were spotted using the restrooms at a gas station near Raton."

My heart quickened. Raton was less than an hour south of Starkville—I'd passed through there only yesterday. The pair were moving back into New Mexico.

Jack continued. "From what we can piece together, they seem to be traveling pretty randomly. Look, Charlie, I'd love to help more, but I can't exactly go chasing them outside of my own jurisdiction. Once the van got towed to Santa Fe, the case kind of left my hands."

"I understand," I said, already pulling up a map on my cell. "Thanks for the info, Jack. I owe you one."

* * *

Although the return trip quickly became boring and routine, the three-hour drive to Raton gave me plenty of time to think. These kids were scared, that much was clear. But there was something else going on here, something that didn't quite add up. The van, stolen in Dallas, the driver murdered, then the drugs and cash, now the erratic movement—it all pointed to a bigger scenario that I was still struggling to see. It was like having all the pieces to a puzzle but not knowing what the finished picture looked like.

As I pulled into Raton, it was already nearing five o'clock. I decided to start with the local motels—if Chelsea and Rory had been in the area, they might have tried to find a place to stay. I aimed for places that were lowkey and inexpensive.

The first two motels were a bust, but at the third, a small, run-down place on the outskirts of town, I struck gold. As I approached the office, I noticed a maid pushing a cleaning cart toward a storage room with a sign— Maintenance. On a hunch, I decided to talk to her first.

"Excuse me," I called out, flashing a friendly smile. "I'm looking for some information. I wonder if you might be able to help me?"

The maid, a middle-aged woman with a wrinkled gray dress and tired eyes, looked at me curiously. "I can try. What do you need to know?"

I pulled out the photos of Chelsea and Rory. "I'm looking for these two. They might have stayed here recently."

The maid studied the photo, then shook her head. "No, I don't think I've seen them. But ..." she hesitated.

"But what?" I prompted gently.

"Well, there was a guy here early this morning. Driving a blue truck. He was asking about a red-headed girl and a guy with tattoos."

I felt a chill run down my spine. This had to be connected. "Can you tell me anything else about this man? Or the truck?"

The maid furrowed her brow in concentration. "The truck was pretty beat up. Older model. And the man ... he seemed agitated. Nervous-like. Kept looking over his shoulder."

I nodded, trying to keep my excitement in check. "Did he stay overnight, or did he move on?"

She shrugged. "No idea."

"Thanks. You've been incredibly helpful."

As I turned to leave, the maid called out. "Oh, I just remembered something else. When the man walked back to his truck, I overheard him talking to someone on his phone. He mentioned something about an 'old Henderson homestead'. It sounded like he was heading there for the night."

I spun back around. "Henderson homestead? Do you

know where that is?"

She shook her head. "No, sorry. But it sounded like it was important to him."

I thanked her again and hurried back to my car. The Henderson homestead—it wasn't much, but it was a lead. And right now, it was the best one I had.

Back on the road, I called Ron. "I need you to look up something for me," I said as soon as he answered. "Any information you can find on an old Henderson homestead in the area around Raton or nearby towns."

I could hear Ron's fingers tapping away at his keyboard. "Give me a few minutes," he said.

While I waited, I mulled over what I knew. A man in a blue truck, looking for a couple who fit their descriptions. It had to be connected to Chelsea and Rory, and this might have something to do with why they were staying on the run. But who was this man? And why was he looking for them?

I thought of the countryside I'd passed through on the way here. This part of the state, east of the Sangre de Cristo mountain range, was fairly flat, lots of farms. Cattle ranches, mostly. It made sense some of them would be original homesteads.

Ron's voice broke into my thoughts. "Okay, I've got something. There's a Henderson farm listed in the Colfax County records. I can't tell whether it's a working ranch anymore, but someone's paying the taxes each year. It's located off highway 58, between Springer and Cimarron."

I'd already started the Jeep and was pulling away from the motel parking lot.

He paused a moment. "Hang on. I've got the property's legal description. Let me see if I can get coordinates for you."

My gut told me this was somehow related. "Thanks. Drop a pin to my phone, Ron." I drove on, watching the exit signs off I-25. When I spotted the highway he'd described, I slowed.

As I exited and drove toward Cimarron, the sun sank below the mountains to the west, plunging the landscape into twilight. The roads became more rural, winding through low hills and grassland. My headlights cut through the growing darkness, illuminating a lonely path where there were few dwellings.

I couldn't shake the feeling that I was racing against time. My gut told me Chelsea and Rory were out here somewhere, possibly in danger. And now there was this mystery man in the blue truck to worry about, asking about them just a few hours ago. The pieces of the puzzle were there, but I still couldn't quite see how they all fit together.

Although the distance was less than sixty miles, I felt as though I was crawling along, looking for the disused turnoff to the Henderson place. Finally, off in the distance, I saw it. A dilapidated barn, silhouetted against the darkening sky. My heart raced as I pulled off the main road onto a rough dirt track leading toward the structure. Recent tire tracks told me I'd found the right place.

As I got closer, I killed the headlights and coasted to a stop beside a scrubby piñon tree, a good distance away from the barn. I didn't want to announce my presence if someone was there. Grabbing my flashlight and pulling my gun from the glovebox, I quietly got out of the Jeep.

The night was eerily silent as I approached the barn, illuminating only the ground at my feet with my flashlight. I stuck with the fresh tire tracks that showed clearly in the dust. As I drew nearer, I could make out more details of the old building. The wood was gray with age, some boards hanging loose. The roof sagged ominously in places.

When a sound broke the silence—a muffled voice coming from inside the barn—I froze, straining my ears. There it was again—definitely a voice, maybe more than one.

My heart pounding, I crept closer to the barn, staying in the shadows. As I reached the wall, I could hear the voices more clearly. Two young voices, speaking lowly and urgently. It had to be Chelsea and Rory.

I took a deep breath, trying to calm my racing thoughts. They were here, alive. But were they alone? Was the man with the blue truck here too?

Carefully, I made my way around the side of the barn, looking for any sign of the blue truck. I didn't see it. In the east wall of the barn, I found a gap between two loose boards and peered inside.

The interior was dark, but I could make out two figures tied to support beams. Chelsea and Rory, looking dirty, scared, and exhausted. My jaw clenched at the sight. Who had done this to them?

Chapter 20

I was about to make my move when I heard the rumble of an engine in the distance. Headlights appeared on the highway, growing brighter as they made the turn toward the old barn.

Quickly, I ducked back into the shadows, my mind racing. This had to be the man with the blue truck. I had to act fast.

I made my way to the barn door, testing it gently. It was unlocked. Taking a deep breath, I pulled it open just enough to slip inside, aiming my flashlight toward the dirt floor.

Chelsea and Rory's heads snapped up at the sound, fear evident in their eyes.

"It's okay," I whispered, hurrying over to them. "I'm

here to help. My name is Charlie Parker. I'm a private investigator."

Relief washed over their faces, quickly replaced by panic as the sound of the approaching vehicle grew louder.

"He's coming back," Chelsea whispered, her voice hoarse with fear.

"Who is he?" I asked, working to untie her bonds.

"Georgie," Rory answered, his voice shaking. "The guy who stole the van. He's after the money."

My mind raced, a few pieces of the puzzle finally clicking into place. The stolen van, the cash, the man in the blue truck—it was beginning to make sense. Somewhat.

As I freed Chelsea and started on Rory's ropes, I heard the vehicle come to a stop right outside. Squeaky truck door slamming. Footsteps approaching.

"Listen to me," I said urgently, working frantically on Rory's bonds. "Stay near your posts, pretend you're still tied up until he's inside. Then, when I tell you to, I want you both to run. My Jeep is parked by a tree, down the road. Go to your right when you get out the door. Get in it and lock the doors. Do you understand?"

They nodded, eyes wide with fear.

Just as Rory's rope came free, the barn door creaked wide open. A man's silhouette appeared in the doorway, backlit by headlights. He took in the scene, spotting me, trying to figure out what was going on.

"What the hell?" He moved toward me, reaching for something at the back of his waistband.

In that moment of his confusion, I made my move. "Run!" I shouted to Chelsea and Rory, simultaneously drawing my gun and aiming my flashlight in Georgie's eyes. "Don't move!" I commanded him.

Chelsea and Rory didn't need to be told twice. They bolted for the door, skirting around Georgie as he stood frozen in shock, trying to shield his eyes from the piercing light.

But the shock didn't last long. With a snarl of rage, Georgie lunged forward, not toward the fleeing teenagers, but toward me.

I squeezed off a warning shot over his left shoulder, the sound deafening in the confined space of the barn. Georgie flinched but didn't stop his charge.

We collided hard, my back slamming against one of the support posts. The impact knocked the wind out of me, and I felt my grip on the gun loosen.

Georgie and I grappled in the darkness, each fighting for control. He was stronger than me, fueled by desperation and rage. But I had training and raw fear on my side.

As we struggled, I caught a glimpse of Chelsea and Rory hovering uncertainly by the barn door. "Go!" I yelled at them. "Get to my Jeep!"

Georgie let out a howl of frustration. In that moment of distraction, I managed to break free from his grip.

Without hesitation, I brought my knee up hard, catching him in the stomach. He doubled over, gasping for air.

I didn't give him a chance to recover. In one fluid motion, I brought my elbow down on the back of his neck. Georgie crumpled to the ground, momentarily stunned.

Not wasting a second, I bolted for the door, my lungs burning as I gulped in the balmy night air. In the distance, I could see Chelsea and Rory running toward my Jeep.

Behind me, I heard Georgie stirring, a string of curses following me into the night. I pushed myself harder, the gap between us and safety feeling impossibly wide.

Chelsea reached the Jeep first, yanking open the passenger door and scrambling inside. Rory was right behind her, practically diving into the backseat.

I could hear Georgie's heavy footsteps behind me, getting closer. My legs felt like lead, but I forced them to keep moving.

Finally, I reached the Jeep, throwing myself into the driver's seat. My hands were shaking as I fumbled with the key fob, acutely aware of Georgie's approaching form in the rearview mirror.

"Come on, come on," I muttered, locking the doors and jamming the key into the ignition.

The engine roared to life just as Georgie reached the Jeep. His face, contorted with rage, appeared at my window. He slammed his fist against the glass, the impact spider-webbing across the window.

"Go!" Chelsea screamed, her voice high with panic.

Well, *yeah* ... I didn't need to be told twice. I threw the Jeep into gear and floored the accelerator. We shot forward, leaving Georgie in a cloud of dust and gravel.

But our escape wasn't clean. In the rearview mirror, I saw Georgie sprinting back to his blue truck. Within moments, headlights flared in my mirrors.

"He's coming," Rory said, his voice shaking as he looked out the back window.

I gritted my teeth, focusing on the winding road ahead. "Buckle up and hold on," I warned, then wrenched the steering wheel to the side.

We veered off the road, plunging into the scrubland. The Jeep bounced and jolted over the uneven terrain, but I switched it into four-wheel drive and kept my foot firmly on the gas.

Behind us, I could hear the roar of Georgie's truck, his headlights probably a hundred yards back. He was following us off-road, apparently not willing to give up his pursuit so easily.

"We need to lose him," I said, my eyes darting between the path ahead and the rearview mirror. "Chelsea, Rory, keep your eyes out for any place we might be able to hide or any path that might be too narrow for his truck."

The next moments were a blur. We tore through the grassland, swerving around cacti and rocks. Although the Jeep's four-wheel drive helped me gain some distance, Georgie's truck stayed stubbornly behind us, its headlights an ever-present threat in our rearview mirrors.

Then, Chelsea spotted it. "There!" she shouted, pointing to our right. "It looks like a riverbed or something!"

I saw it too—a deep cut in the earth, barely visible in the dark. It was risky, but it might be our only chance.

"Hang on tight," I warned, then cranked the wheel hard to the right.

We skidded toward the arroyo, dust billowing around us. For a heart-stopping moment, I thought we might not make it. But then the Jeep's tires found purchase, and we dove down into the shadows.

I killed the headlights, plunging us into near-total darkness. We crept forward slowly, the edges of the arroyo close on either side.

Above us, we heard the roar of Georgie's truck as it shot past our hiding spot. The sound faded into the distance, and then ... silence. I opened my door and stood on the floorboard, stretching to see over the rim of the arroyo. In the distance, a set of headlights headed west, toward Cimarron.

We all held our breath, straining our ears for any sign that Georgie had discovered our trick and was waiting to leap out of the dark. But there was nothing but the quiet of the desert night.

After what felt like an eternity, I let out a shaky breath. "I think we lost him," I said softly.

Chelsea and Rory sagged in their seats, the tension draining out of them. I could hear muffled sobs from the passenger seat as the reality of their ordeal hit home.

"Everything we own is in our packs," Rory moaned.

Chelsea sniffed loudly. "Almost everything. I've got my dead cell phone."

Rory actually smiled at that. "And thank goodness we always kept our wallets in our pockets. So, we can come up with two or three whole dollars if we have to." Humor in the face of a near-tragedy. At least that was something.

"It's okay," I said, trying to keep my voice calm and reassuring despite my own racing heart. "You're safe now. We're going to get out of here, and then we'll figure out what to do next."

I started the Jeep moving again, slowly navigating out of the ravine. Once we were back on somewhat level ground, I debated which direction to take. If those had been Georgie's headlights heading west, he would soon reach Cimarron, a small town with a rich Old West history but nothing in the way of nightlife. People there would typically settle in at home and the few stores and restaurants would soon be closing. We didn't want to stand out, and I most certainly didn't want to be one of only two vehicles on the lonely stretch of road beyond it. I pointed us eastward, toward the interstate.

Once we'd joined the steady southbound flow of traffic on I-25, I finally felt as though I could catch my breath. I glanced toward the passenger seat and saw Chelsea had fallen asleep with her head against the window. In the back, Rory was curled up in the spot where Freckles usually rides. Stretching my arms and shoulders, I smiled, relieved that I'd found them.

My smile faded a little when I realized it was well after sundown and I hadn't heard from Drake today. Not that a call was a must-do for us, but we normally did touch base at the end of each day, especially when he was doing dangerous work. Dangerous work—I almost sputtered. What I'd just dashed into had been pretty darn scary.

I picked up my phone and broke one of my cardinal driving rules when I held it to my ear as the call went to voicemail. I kept my voice low, conscious of my napping companions. "Hey, just checking in, hoping everything's okay out there. I'll be awake for a while yet, so give me a call back."

I told myself there were a dozen reasons he might not pick up the phone—everything from low battery to grabbing a late supper to being in the shower. Surely, I would hear from him soon. I forced myself to relax and for the next hour, I simply enjoyed the silence in the car.

In the back, Rory began to stir, sitting up and scrubbing at his face with grimy hands. He spotted the next exit sign. "Vegas? We've come that far already?"

Chelsea immediately came awake and smiled. "It's Las Vegas, New Mexico, dweeb."

"Around here we refer to it as the *original* Las Vegas," I offered.

"It's like a hundred and thirty years older than the glitzy

one," Chelsea informed him, turning to face the back seat. "There's a ton of history there. Doc Holliday, Wyatt Earp … lots of those famous men spent time here. The Santa Fe Railroad and the Santa Fe Trail come through here, the Harvey Hotel chain …"

"I can tell you were a good student, Chelsea," I told her with a smile.

She shrugged. "I always liked history."

I let a few more miles go by as we passed through the old town, heading toward Albuquerque. "Look, guys, do you mind if I ask some questions? You're going to face them soon enough anyway. The yellow van—the police have it. They know you abandoned it in Santa Rosa. What I'm wondering is, where along the way did you take it? Was it in Dallas?"

"Dallas? Heck no." Rory was leaning forward now. "We were in Austin, trying to line up some work with a band. That didn't exactly pan out, so we decided to head for Vegas. Um, the one that's got all the casinos and stuff."

Chelsea reached through the space between the front seats and laid a hand on his arm. "That horrible guy, Georgie, he picked us up outside Lubbock. He was pretty nice at first, said he was on the way to visit a cousin in Albuquerque."

"This Georgie … did he give you a last name?"

"Um, I'm pretty sure he said it was Lafarge." Chelsea nodded to confirm Rory's guess.

"Hold on a minute. I want to get someone on this." I got on the hands-free app for my phone and told it to call Ron, belatedly realizing it was after ten p.m. already.

"Hey, this better be good," he grumped as he answered.

"It is." I gave him the basics, how I had Chelsea and

Rory with me, and asked him to find out all he could about a Georgie Lafarge, including whether this was someone John Flick would know.

"Tomorrow okay with you?'

I laughed. "Tomorrow's fine." I ended the call and turned to my passengers. "Okay, the rest of the story, please."

It came out in bits and pieces. The initial thrill of adventure, the shock of discovering the van's contents, their desperate attempts to stay ahead of both Georgie and the law. Chelsea was crying by the time she finished, saying she just wanted to go home.

My heart ached for these two young people who had made some monumentally bad decisions. But they were so young. Scared, remorseful, and in desperate need of help.

"Listen," I said making eye contact with each of them. "You're not in trouble with me. But we have to figure out what to do next. I promise I'll be with you every step of the way, okay? Are you hungry?"

They nodded, a glimmer of hope on their tear-stained faces.

It was after eleven as we approached the Bernalillo exit. I pulled into the parking lot of a 24-hour Denny's, finally allowing myself to relax slightly.

"Okay," I said, turning to face Chelsea and Rory. "We're safe for now, but we've got some decisions to make. Are you ready to talk about what happens next?"

They exchanged a look, then nodded solemnly.

Chapter 21

My phone rang about two seconds after their omelets were brought to the table. I jumped, grabbing the phone in hopes that it was Drake. Rory and Chelsea dug into their food as I took the call from an unfamiliar number.

"Charlie Parker," I answered.

"Ms. Parker, this is Beth Watson. I ... I know it's late and I hope I'm not bothering you." The voice on the other end sounded nervous, hesitant.

"Not at all, Ms. Watson. What can I do for you?"

There was a pause, then Beth continued, her words tumbling out in a rush. "I used to work for Flick Helicopters in Galveston. I saw on a newsfeed that authorities are looking for information about a missing vehicle from there. It caught my attention because, well, I think I might know something about it. But I'm afraid to contact the police directly, especially those in Galveston. I don't know who I can trust."

My interest was immediately piqued. "I understand, Ms. Watson. Can you tell me more?"

"It's a lot to go into over the phone," she replied quickly. "But I'm in Albuquerque right now. Is there any chance we could meet in person?"

I considered for a moment. This could be the break we needed, but I was afraid to leave Chelsea and Rory alone. "Things are a little crazy right now," I said finally. "Can I call you back with a time and place once I've sorted out a few things. Is that all right?"

Beth agreed, and I ended the call, my mind already spinning with possibilities. What did Beth know about Flick's business? And how did it connect to the stolen van and the contraband aboard it?

"Everything okay?" Chelsea asked as she spread jam on her toast.

"It will be." But I had no idea whether that was true or not.

Georgie Lafarge was still out there somewhere, and I had no doubt he'd be looking for us. He needed to know what the young couple had done with the drugs and cash from the van. We needed a safe place to regroup and figure out our next move. That's when it hit me—my own home in Albuquerque. It might not be an ideal safehouse, but it was the best option we had right now.

I scanned the parking lot outside the restaurant, alert to every new vehicle that pulled in. I saw no sign of the blue pickup truck, but it didn't mean Georgie hadn't swapped it for something else along the way.

My charges blazed through their meals in record time

and I guessed they'd not had much to eat in recent days. My stomach was way too knotted up to handle food; I'd ordered one pancake and barely finished half of it. I rechecked the parking lot before we walked out into the night, instructing them not to linger. I wanted all of us locked in the Jeep and back on the move.

The short remaining drive into Albuquerque had never felt so long. Every vehicle that appeared in my mirrors sent a jolt of anxiety through me. Was it Georgie? Had he had time to catch up with us and somehow find us? But each time, it turned out to be just another traveler on the road.

As I drove, I outlined the plan I had in mind, telling Rory and Chelsea that I would take them to my house, where we had a comfortable guest room. I could come up with spare toothbrushes and some clean clothing, since their backpacks had been abandoned in the process of escaping their captor. Chelsea reached under her shirt and pulled out a cell phone she'd tucked into her waistband. "It's dead and my charger is gone, but at least creepy Georgie didn't find it."

"Ah, good thinking," I said.

I took a circuitous route through town, watching my mirrors. An occasional vehicle showed up behind me but they never followed, so I felt safe by the time I reached my own neighborhood. When I came to our driveway, I hit the brakes in shock. Drake's truck was home.

He always left it at Double Eagle, the small westside airport, when he left for a job. Why wasn't he in Arizona?

As I pulled into my driveway, I turned to face Rory and Chelsea. "Listen, I know this isn't ideal, but you'll be safe here while I figure out our next steps. Just remember, you need to lay low, okay?"

They nodded, relief evident in their tired eyes. I ushered them inside, introducing them to Drake and Freckles, showing them to the guest room and making sure they had everything they needed. Once they were settled, I turned to Drake, my eyes full of questions.

"You're home—is the fire out?"

"No such luck. I had to get the ship back for the hundred-hour inspection. Can't believe how much we're flying on this job, but I knew this was coming up." He pulled me into a hug that reeked of woodsmoke.

When I gave a discreet cough, he pulled back. "Sorry. I really want a shower and fresh clothes, and then I want to hear about your day."

Um, you probably don't. But I would cover that later. I gave him a playful shove toward our bathroom, while I retreated to the kitchen to make a phone call. I'd nearly forgotten that one of Flick's employees—*former* employee—had reached out to me earlier. I didn't want to leave Ms. Watson hanging for too long.

"Beth? It's Charlie Parker again. Can you meet me in the morning at Manny's—seven o'clock?" I chose the popular eatery in the university area over something more isolated, since I really didn't know this woman.

She readily agreed and said she was familiar with the area. Once the call ended, I stood in the middle of the kitchen, trying to gather my thoughts and figure out what to do next. All the lights were out at Elsa's, which I hoped was a good sign. I hadn't found even a moment to call her during the afternoon.

When I looked around, Drake stood in the kitchen doorway, glancing over his shoulder toward the short hall that led to the guest room. He had his phone in his hand.

"Sorry I didn't hear your calls come in earlier. I guess you were worried about me while I was worrying about you."

We shared a weak laugh over that. "Want to fill me in?"

I did, minimizing the scene in the old barn where I'd been half terrified out of my wits. "I think Chelsea and Rory want to get back home to California, but I need to have them talk to Ron—and maybe the police—before I let go of them. They may be able to fill in details that will help us piece together what was behind the theft of the van and why it happened to be carrying a bunch of drugs and cash."

During all this, my wonderful hubby had brewed me a cup of chamomile tea and we sat at the kitchen table. I finally felt some of the electrical tension ease out of my body.

I finished my tea and went to our room to gather a few items of clothing. My jeans would come close enough to fitting Chelsea, even though she was a couple inches shorter. And I thought Rory could get by with a pair of Drake's sweats and a t-shirt, at least until we could launder their own clothes. I stacked my charitable little stash in the guest bathroom after peeking into the bedroom where I saw they were completely zonked out.

Drake rechecked all the locks and got Freckles settled into her bed with a cookie while I took a quick shower. It felt good to lie down beside him at the end of such a long day.

"What's the status with your job?" I asked, keeping my voice low in the darkness.

"The fire is less than ten percent contained, and they've put all resources on it. My inspection is the only reason I've broken away for even a few hours. Once Steve finishes the hundred-hour, I'll be due back in Arizona. He'll probably have the whole inspection done by noon."

"Do you mind sticking around here until mid-morning? Not that I distrust our young guests, but …"

"We really don't know them," he finished. "You got it."

I snuggled into his shoulder, cherishing his presence. If there was any way to keep him from going back, I'd do it. But I also knew there were severe penalties for breaking the contract.

* * *

Pale dawn light began to show at the windows around five, and I immediately came awake. Our guests were just beginning to stir, and Drake already had a good start on breakfast for them with a big batch of pancake batter. At six forty-five, I headed out, leaving strict instructions with Chelsea and Rory to stay put and call me immediately if anything seemed off.

The university area came alive early in the day and Manny's was bustling, everyone else wrapped up in their own conversations—perfect for a discreet meeting. I spotted my contact as soon as I walked in. She was sitting in a corner booth, nervously fidgeting with a manila envelope in front of her. I made my way over.

"Beth? I'm Charlie Parker. Thank you for meeting me."

Beth nodded as I slid into the seat opposite, her eyes darting around the restaurant before settling on me. "Thank you for coming. I … I wasn't sure who else to turn to."

"How did you know to reach out to me, specifically?"

A waitress appeared at our table, carafe in hand, and we both accepted coffee.

"Ah. Well, a friend I worked with at Flick Helicopters was at the convention a couple weeks ago. She saw Mr. Flick and Harrison talking with you and your husband, and Mr. Flick said he'd made an appointment with a private investigator." Beth stirred sugar into her mug. "I kind of wormed your name out of her after she related that story."

"And you traveled to Albuquerque to meet me?"

"Actually, my parents live here. It's where I came after I lost my job. I already have another one." She glanced at her watch and relaxed back into her seat.

"So, this information you've got. Why don't you start at the beginning?" I suggested gently. "Tell me about your time at Flick Helicopters."

Beth took a deep breath, then began her story. She had worked as an accountant for Flick Helicopters for three years. At first, everything seemed normal, but over time, she started noticing discrepancies in the books.

"There were large sums of money coming in that didn't match up with our contracts," she explained. "And then there were these strange shipping manifests. Items that didn't make sense for a helicopter company. The general manager, Harrison Stoker, signed a lot of them, but Mr. Flick's name was on there too."

"These weren't one-time deliveries?"

She shook her head. "I started digging, translating code words they used for stuff. A lot of the fake manifests were written in Spanish," Beth continued, lowering her voice.

Cartels. This was heavy-duty stuff.

"I'm pretty sure I found evidence of money laundering, drug trafficking, maybe even weapons smuggling. When Mr. Flick realized I was onto all this, he had Harrison fire me. But not before I managed to make copies of some key documents."

She slid the manila envelope across the table to me. "It's all in here. I made copies of bank statements, shipping records, everything. I was too scared to go to the police in Galveston. I don't know how far this corruption goes."

"Do you recognize the name Georgie Lafarge? Or maybe it's George?"

Her brow furrowed for a moment but she shook her head. "I don't think I ever came across that name."

I'd have to figure out the connection at some point.

I took the envelope, my heart racing with the implications of what it contained. "Wow. This sounds major. You did the right thing, Beth. This could explain a lot."

Her shoulders sagged with relief. "What happens now?"

"Now, I take this to some trusted contacts in the DEA and local police," I said, carefully tucking the envelope into my bag. "Your information could be the key to bringing the whole thing down. Are you willing to testify if it comes to that?"

Beth hesitated for a moment, then nodded resolutely. "Yes. It's time someone stood up to them."

We talked for a while longer, going over the details of what Beth had discovered. By the time we parted ways, my mind was buzzing with the new information. This seemed way bigger than I would have guessed. The evidence Beth had provided could be the missing link we needed to connect all the dots. But I still couldn't figure out why John Flick would have hired us if he was fully aware of what that van contained.

I drove home, feeling nervous. We were close—so close to unraveling this whole twisted mess, but I was missing some major clue.

Pulling into my driveway, a nagging worry crept in, worry over having Rory and Chelsea under my roof. Georgie Lafarge was still out there, and now we knew we were dealing with an entire criminal organization. This case was far from over, and the stakes had just gotten a lot higher.

Chapter 22

I entered the house to be greeted enthusiastically by Freckles. I rubbed her ears and gave her a kiss on the forehead. I could hear Drake in the kitchen, where it sounded as if he was on the phone. As I passed the guest room, I heard muffled voices. I paused, listening.

"We can't stay here forever, Rory," Chelsea was saying, her voice tight with worry. "What are we going to do?"

"I don't know," Rory replied, sounding defeated. "But Charlie's helping us. Maybe ... maybe it'll be okay."

I moved away from the door, my heart heavy. This couple had been through so much, and their ordeal wasn't over yet. But hearing Rory's words—his trust in me—strengthened my resolve to see this through, to dig out the truth.

In my bedroom, I opened the envelope Beth had given me. Bank statements showing large deposits. Shipping manifests with coded entries that didn't match any legitimate helicopter parts. But those deposits could be payments for big jobs, and the entries could be anything. I was only taking Beth's word for it that they weren't business related. It could be a goldmine of evidence, but it would take time to analyze fully.

Drake walked in. "Hey, I didn't know you were back."

I showed him a couple of the pages. "John Flick flies some of the same aircraft you do—can you tell if these part numbers match up?"

He studied the line items for a full minute. "I don't think so. But you know how it is—they've got it so complex that every model has a whole parts list of its own." He gave me a website name where I could look them up, in case the manufacturer had come up with something different, something specific to different machines.

While I jotted it down, he walked to the closet and pulled out a clean flight suit. "That was Steve on the phone just now. Inspection's done and we're ready for an engine run-up. Then I've gotta get back on the job. Fires wait for no one."

"Anything I can do to help?" *Such as locking you in a closet and lying like hell to keep you at home.*

He shook his head as he zipped up his suit. "Just give me a kiss and hope we get this thing under control soon. Praying for rain never hurts either."

I did all that, turning to hide the moisture in my eyes as he walked out the door and got in his truck.

I took a deep breath and then went to check on my houseguests. Chelsea walked into the hall as I arrived, dressed in a pair of shorts and t-shirt I'd loaned her the night before. She gave me a timid smile.

"Drake showed us where the washer and dryer are, and we got our clothes cleaned up."

"Good. I can loan you some more things, if you need them. I feel badly that your backpacks got lost along the way."

"Yeah, somewhere in Georgie's stolen truck, I suppose." She bit her lower lip. "There were a few things in there I'll miss … but I feel lucky we got out of that mess alive."

I reached out and squeezed her hand. "It'll work out okay. Look, I need to get to my office, and I'm thinking this would be a good chance for us to find out what you and Rory need to do next. I'm sure the police will need a statement, and maybe the DEA as well."

She glanced over her shoulder toward the guest room.

"I'll be right there with you, wherever you need to be. And then I guess we need to talk about getting you guys home. That is, if home is where you want to be."

She didn't answer. I got the feeling this was a source of friction between them.

As she headed toward the laundry room to get clothes from the dryer, I remembered my conversations with each of their parents. I could understand Rory's hesitance.

Twenty minutes later, with everyone dressed in jeans and clean shirts, we piled into the Jeep and headed for RJP. Sally had been briefed, and she immediately went into mothering mode, offering sodas, juices, snacks, and donuts that had somehow magically appeared in the office cupboards. Chelsea passed up everything, for now she said, and Rory accepted a Coke.

Ron came downstairs, and I made the introductions all around.

"Ron's the one who has been behind the scenes all along, tracking vehicle IDs and more," I assured them.

Chelsea's eyes moistened. "We had no idea ... I mean, it really felt like we were all alone out there."

Remembering the look on her face when I'd entered that barn last night, I knew what she meant. It had been a frightening time, from the start.

"I've got a call to make. Sally will take good care of you if you want something to eat or drink." I headed up to my office and closed the door as I pulled my phone out and found the number I'd been given for the Albuquerque DEA field office.

Once I had Oliver Gant on the line, I introduced myself and gave a brief context of what I was calling about. "I was contacted by a former employee of Flick Helicopters, who gave me some documentation that pertains to the case you're building. And I've got the young couple who ended up with the van that was stolen from the company."

"Can we meet this afternoon?" he asked.

"Certainly. Would it be possible for you to come to our offices? We're not far from downtown, but I'm thinking our young witnesses would be more comfortable if they aren't walking into the Federal building."

He said he would be here at two o'clock.

After setting up the meeting, I leaned back in my chair, my mind whirling with details. I pulled out a pad and began making notes on what we knew, from the search for a stolen van, then the missing young couple, to the discovery of the drug operation, the missing money—it still wasn't quite fitting together. I had a feeling Chelsea and Rory held more of the pieces, which would help solve it, but they didn't really know what we needed yet. Neither did I.

I walked back downstairs to inform Ron about the meeting and found our charges set up in the conference room with the TV on and a bowl of popcorn between them. Sally was keeping a vigilant eye, telling me she'd locked the doors, in case 'that crazy dude' should show up and try to just walk in.

"Where's Ron?"

"Went out for burgers. He figured it's best to keep them under our wing here, so he's bringing lunch for all."

"Good plan. We'll have some law enforcement help soon, I think."

I caught myself checking my phone, knowing Drake should have arrived at the fire base camp and would be sending a text to confirm that, at any minute. But nothing came.

At five minutes before two, a gray sedan pulled up to the curb out front, a vehicle so plain that it screamed 'federal agents.' Out climbed two people, a man who would easily be cast for the role of a DEA agent in a movie—tall, sandy hair neatly cut, a dark suit with a white shirt and tie. His companion was a woman about my size and build, wearing the same uniform—skirted version. Her dark hair was in a tight bun at her neck. They both adjusted their sunglasses (of course they did) and walked up the sidewalk to our front door.

Sally, bless her, asked them to show their IDs through the glass before she unlocked the door. Then she showed them in. I had closed the door to the conference room and instructed Rory and Chelsea to wait quietly until we knew what was what. Once we were certain that Oliver Gant and Melanie Baca were who they claimed to be, I ushered them into the conference room and introduced everyone. Ron took the seat at the head of the table and the others chose places.

"Charlie, you want to start this off?" Gant requested.

From across the table, I slid Beth's manila envelope over to him.

"This is everything Beth Watson collected during her time at Flick Helicopters," I explained as Gant began to examine the documents. "Bank statements, shipping manifests, internal memos—it's all there."

His eyebrows rose higher with each page he turned, as Baca looked on. "This is … significant, Charlie. If this checks out, we're looking at a major drug trafficking operation, possibly weapons smuggling too."

I nodded, feeling a mix of excitement and apprehension. "What's the next step?"

"We'll need to verify everything, of course," Gant said, carefully returning the documents to the envelope. "But if it all pans out, we'll be looking at multiple arrests, possibly international warrants."

He tucked the envelope into his briefcase and turned to face Chelsea and Rory for the first time. "Do you mind answering some questions here, or would you rather come to our offices? Either way is fine with us." He wore a smile, as did Agent Baca, but the meaning was clear enough. The government wanted answers.

Chelsea responded for both of them. "Here is fine."

Melanie Baca leaned forward and I wondered if this was the beginning of a game of good-cop, bad-cop. If so, she was clearly playing the good-cop role. "We hear that you two have really been through the wringer this week. So, all we really need is to hear how it happened. In your own words, how did you come to be driving that yellow van?"

Chelsea straightened and took a long breath. "We were hitchhiking. The van stopped and the guy offered a ride. It was so hot out and we both just had to get off our feet."

"Yeah, we were completely beat." Rory leaned a little closer to his girlfriend.

"So, anyway, he seemed nice enough …"

"His name?" Gant had a notepad out now.

"He said it was George Lafarge—Georgie. Said he was on the way to visit a cousin in Albuquerque."

During the next few minutes they repeated things they'd already told me. Georgie had stopped for the night at a motel and they got a little creeped out about that, and when they discovered the keys were in the van, they just stole it and took off.

"I know it wasn't right," Chelsea said. "We should have just caught another ride and left him—"

"Left him and the damn van behind," Rory added. "I don't know why—I can't really explain—"

Gant interrupted. "Tell us what you found in the back of the van. Everything."

"At first, just some tools and greasy rags, stuff a mechanic might use, I guess." Rory scratched his head and turned toward Chelsea.

"We had our backpacks with us, and figured we'd pull over somewhere and sleep, but then the van started running rough and it completely conked out. We were almost into Santa Rosa, and we coasted to a stop when it quit. We slept in there, and in the morning Rory started looking through stuff to see if we could find anything that would help. It wasn't like we could just get a garage guy to come out and fix it for us."

Melanie nodded sympathetically.

"There was a loose panel on the inside and we opened it up and then it was like, oh shit, and we didn't know what to do with the stuff."

"Stuff?"

"Pills. There were big bundles of them, wrapped up like they might be if they were for sale, and the whole mess was wrapped in layers of plastic, and I just got *so* scared." Chelsea's voice began shaking.

"Did you know what they were?"

Rory took over again. "Not right away, but then we wondered if it could be fentanyl, and I've heard it's really nasty and Chels said we didn't dare get caught with it. So, we divided up the packages and when we walked into town a little later, we dumped one or two packets into various dumpsters."

"It's probably already in the landfill, or wherever they take the garbage around there," Chelsea added.

"Okay, you got rid of all the drugs that way?"

Nods from both.

"Anything else back there, in the van?"

The two young people exchanged a glance, and Chelsea spoke. "Cash. Bundles of hundred-dollar bills. I didn't actually count it, but there was a lot. Like probably fifty or sixty bundles."

"And what did you do with that?"

"We carried it with us, in our packs, for a while but we got worried about either getting caught with it or getting robbed. They were really crisp, new bills. We spent one of them on some food at a place and Rory was going to buy some parts to fix the van, but we got the stink-eye from this dude who clearly wondered about us."

"Yeah, that kinda scared us off from trying to spend any more of it."

"So, where's the cash now?" Melanie seemed genuinely curious, as if she was reading all this in a gripping novel.

Again, a shared look between the two. Meanwhile, all the rest of us were a rapt audience. Even Sally was leaning against the doorjamb, staring, despite the fact that she would have normally gone home more than an hour ago.

"You tell it," Rory said, an impish grin on his face.

Chelsea played to the audience. "Trinidad."

"That's it?" I admit it, I was hooked. "Like, all over Trinidad?"

She shook her head. "No, that would have made the news." She reached for Rory's hand. "Once we decided to leave his uncle's cabin, we had no idea what to do next. And I suggested we just turn it in to the police and get rid of it. But that would lead to questions and the police might hold us, and that guy Georgie might come along and claim he was bailing us out or something, so …"

Chapter 23

Oliver Gant slammed his pen down on the table. "Quit playing around. So, you did what?"

"We put it in the bank."

"And how did you do that?" Ron asked. "You deposited it? In your own account?"

"Yes, kinda. And no." Chelsea was enjoying herself, this game of storytelling.

Rory finally caved and gave away the ending. "We dropped it into a night deposit thingy."

"Yeah, it was a really old bank building, and on the outside was a metal door that said something like Night Depository ... something like that. We just started stuffing packets in there, lifting the handle, hearing it drop. Doing it all over again until we were rid of the money." She shifted in her chair. "Wait … you didn't know about this? No one at the bank put the word out that a bunch of money just showed up?"

"We'll check our sources, young lady. You can bet we'll be following up and checking out your story."

I almost felt sorry for the federal agents, knowing they had an impossible trail to the drugs and a rather dubious one, considering chain of custody and all, to the cash. I verified with Gant that he would do as Peterson had told me, share the information from their interview with the New Mexico State Police. He agreed. As the agents left our office, I felt a weight lift off my shoulders. Beth's evidence was in the right hands now. They knew the story about the rest of it.

The finish line was getting closer, but there were still loose ends to tie up. Who killed Ben Estevez, the mechanic, and where was Evil George? And, perhaps most puzzling of all, why would John Flick have hired us if he was running drugs and illicit cash through his helicopter business? I knew better than to pose these questions to the feds; they wouldn't know either. Bringing up new subjects would only complicate the day further, and my head was pounding already.

I saw the two DEA agents out the door, while Sally tidied up the office kitchen and Ron disappeared into his office. Too tired to think about cooking, which isn't my strong point anyway, I phoned a pizza order to our favorite place. Freckles and I, along with Rory and Chelsea, picked it up and took it home.

Belatedly, I remembered to check my messages but there was still nothing from Drake. I tried his number but it went straight to voicemail.

Exhaustion settled over us as we consumed the

pepperoni pizza at my kitchen table. I sensed that both of my guests felt talked-out. I certainly did, and I wasn't ready to bring up any more heavy-duty topics tonight. I halfheartedly ate one slice but found I had one ear tuned for my phone.

Excusing myself, I walked over to check on Elsa, thinking I should have invited her over to share the pizza, but frankly I'd been too tired to play hostess any more than I absolutely had to. When I inquired about whether she had heard anything from Dottie today, she shook her head.

"Not a peep. I sure hope things are going okay with her daughter. Dottie has nursing experience, you know. She could end up being the one to stay and give medical care through the whole pregnancy."

Would that put Ron and me in the position of having to find a new caregiver for Elsa? It was a tricky situation. She'd had a heart attack a couple years ago, and at her age really shouldn't be all alone. None of us wanted to see her go into a nursing home, and we'd been oh so lucky to find Dottie because she wasn't asking the sky-high rates of most caregivers provided by agencies. If she didn't come back, this could turn into a real pickle.

I told Gram to call me if she needed anything at all. When she mentioned she'd seen two extra people come home with me last night, I covered by saying they were some friends who were staying a day or so. There was no way I wanted her having information that could be tortured out of her. She needed to remain an innocent in all this.

In the kitchen, the kids were putting away the leftover slices, and the excited clicking of Freckles's nails on the floor told me she was right with them, hoping for a handout of some kind. I gave her a pat on the head and went to my bedroom to see whether I needed to launder Drake's smoky flight suit, the one he'd exchanged for a clean one.

I'd just dropped some clothes into the washer when I looked up to see Chelsea standing by the door. I wasn't unhappy when she told me they were ready to call it a night. It must be a challenge for people their age to entertain themselves without their cell phones, and it reminded me I hadn't offered to find a charger for hers. Rory's phone was apparently gone for good.

I wished them both a restful night and watched them retreat to their room, then I made the rounds to double-check the door and window locks before turning out the lights and heading for my own comfy bed. Freckles trotted along behind me the whole way.

* * *

The trill of my phone jolted me awake. I fumbled for it in the dark, squinting at the numerals when they lit up. 5:34 a.m. The phone number was an unfamiliar one. This couldn't be good news.

"Charlie Parker," I answered, my voice still rough with sleep.

"You listen to me, you nosy bitch," a male voice snarled through the speaker.

I was instantly alert, fumbling for the lamp switch and struggling to recognize the voice.

"You and that partner of yours need to butt out of our business, or things are going to get real unpleasant real quick."

Business. Flick. But it wasn't his voice. I sat up, my mind racing. Then it clicked. The chief pilot and general manager, Harrison Stoker.

"Mr. Stoker, I'm not sure what you're talking about. John is the one who hired us to locate your missing van, remember?"

His laugh was cold and humorless. "And you found it. Now, you've been poking around where you don't belong. You've got something that belongs to me, and I want it back. You've got twenty-four hours to return it and forget everything you've learned, or you'll regret it."

Well, that wasn't happening. But before I could respond, the line went dead. I stared at the phone for a moment, processing what had just happened. He must be referring to the cash and the drugs. The irony wasn't lost on me—the righthand man for the company who had hired us to find their van was now threatening us to stop our investigation. If I needed any more confirmation that we were on the right track, this was it.

Tossing my phone onto the duvet, I finally got the lamp to turn on. Freckles looked up from her bed on the floor, looking as muddled as I felt. I grabbed my robe and slipped it on, even as I wondered whether I was the only one to receive a call like this.

I quickly dialed Ron's number, relieved when he answered on the second ring. "Ron, it's Charlie. Are you okay?"

"Yeah, I'm fine," he replied, sounding confused. "What's going on?"

I filled him in on Stoker's call, hearing his sharp intake of breath. "No, I didn't hear from them," he said when I finished. "I'd treat a threat like this as serious, Charlie."

"I know," I agreed. "But we're close, Ron. I can feel it. I'm just relieved we already turned over Beth's evidence to the DEA. Hopefully they'll come up with the break in the case and we'll be off the hook entirely."

After reminding Ron to stay safe and keep his eyes open, I hung up and got dressed. The house was quiet as I made my way to the kitchen; Chelsea and Rory were still asleep in the guest room. I started the coffee maker and took Freckles out to the back yard. Once she'd finished her businesses, I fed her and poured my first cup.

As I sipped my coffee, I couldn't help but feel a renewed determination. Flick's threats—because I had to believe this threat came from the top—only proved we were on the right track, and I was more resolved than ever to see this thing through to the end. I itched to call him back and tell him what had really happened to the drugs and the cash, but that would only tip our hand and give away the fact that this was now a federal case. I couldn't risk Flick trying to escape, at this point. I sighed and rinsed my cup.

When I left the kitchen, I found Chelsea and Rory in the living room, talking quietly. They looked up as I entered, their expressions nervous.

"Hey," I said, taking a chair across from them. "I think it's time we had a talk."

They exchanged a glance before Chelsea spoke. "Are … are we in trouble with the police?"

I shook my head. "I don't think so. Okay, maybe minimal because of taking the van from that Georgie person." And maybe disposing of evidence, and maybe some other stuff, too. I didn't say that. "But now we need to discuss what happens next." I took a deep breath, choosing my words carefully. "I know you've been through a lot, and I understand why you ran away. But it's time to think about going home."

Rory's mouth tightened. "I can't," he whispered. "My dad … he won't understand."

"Your dad isn't happy with the choices you made. I suspect maybe *you* aren't happy with some of those choices either. Give it a chance. He might surprise you, and maybe he'll come around," I said gently, looking toward each of them. "They've been worried sick about you. Both of your families have."

Rory reached out and took Chelsea's hand. "Maybe Charlie's right, Chels. I'm … I'm tired of running. Of being scared all the time."

Chelsea nodded, wiping her eyes. "Me too. I'm so tired of all of this. Of dealing with people like Georgie."

At the mention of Georgie's name, I saw something flash in their eyes. "What is it?" I prompted. "Is there something you haven't told me about this guy?"

They exchanged another look, and this time it was Rory who spoke. "Georgie … he killed someone. The guy whose license we found, Benjamin Estevez."

I felt my blood run cold. "Are you sure?"

Chelsea nodded, her face pale. "We overheard him talking about it. He was bragging to someone on the phone."

I leaned forward, my mind racing. "This is important information. Can you tell me anything else about Georgie? Anything that might help us find him?"

Rory's brow furrowed in concentration. "The blue truck he was driving … I remember the license plate. It was KLM-5697. New Mexico."

I immediately pulled out my phone, dialing Ron's number, reporting the license plate and relaying the information about Benjamin Estevez. "Get that out to whoever needs to know—local and state police, DEA ... whoever."

I turned back to Chelsea and Rory. "Thank you," I said sincerely. "This will help to solve a big part of this mystery. What you've told me could be crucial in catching and bringing Georgie to justice."

Chelsea managed a small smile. "Really?"

I nodded. "Really. Now, about your families ..."

We spent the next hour talking through their fears and concerns. I listened as Chelsea opened up about the pressure she felt from her parents, and how Rory had seemed like an escape from all of that.

Rory agreed, sharing his own insecurities and how he'd gotten caught up in the excitement of their adventure without fully considering the consequences. "Maybe college wouldn't be such a bad plan, I guess."

As they talked, I could see the weight lifting from their shoulders. They were just kids who had made some bad decisions, caught up in something much bigger and more dangerous than they could have ever imagined.

"Look," I said when they had finished. "I can't promise that everything will be easy when you go home. There will be tough conversations, probably some arguments. But I can promise you this—your parents love you. They want you safe. And working things out with them has got to be better than constantly looking over your shoulder, wondering if a slimeball like Georgie or thugs from a drug cartel are going to catch up with you."

Chelsea wiped her eyes and nodded. "You're right. I ... I want to go home. I want to try to fix things."

Rory squeezed her hand. "I'll give it a try. But it doesn't mean I'm giving up on my dreams about the music business, and I'm going to be right upfront with my dad about that."

I felt a surge of relief. "That's good. That's really good. We'll make the calls today, okay? But first, there's one more thing."

I explained about the how the evidence would move through the legal system, and the likely court proceedings that would follow. "You'll probably be asked to make statements," I told them. "About what you saw, what you overheard. It won't be easy, but it's important. You can help put some very bad people away."

They looked scared but determined. "We'll do it," Rory said, Chelsea nodding in agreement.

As I looked at these two, I felt a fierce protectiveness wash over me—they'd been through so much. They had made mistakes, yes, but they had also shown courage and resilience in the face of danger. They deserved a chance to make things right. I'd found them and brought them in; I didn't want the rest of this journey to backfire on them.

That uncertainty, plus the fact that it was now close to twenty-four hours since I'd heard from Drake, niggled at the edges of my thoughts. I shook it off. Taking action was always better than worrying.

"Okay," I said, standing up. "Let's make those calls to your parents. Then we'll talk about next steps."

I couldn't help but feel that we were turning a corner in this case. The evidence was with the DEA, Georgie's description and vehicle information were with the police, and Chelsea and Rory were ready to face the music and go home.

But even as I felt a sense of progress, I knew we weren't out of the woods yet. Stoker's threatening call this morning was a stark reminder that there were still dangerous people out there, people who wouldn't hesitate to hurt us to protect their interests. And we still didn't know if Georgie Lafarge had gone away for good.

As I heard the phone ringing, waiting for Chelsea's parents to answer, I made a silent vow. I would see this through to the end, for those many lives that had been touched by this case.

The voice of Chelsea's mother answered, thick with emotion, and I took a deep breath. "Mrs. Brown, this is Charlie Parker. I have some good news."

I handed the phone over, feeling a lump in my throat.

"Mom? It's me …"

Chapter 24

From the kitchen, I could hear bits of Chelsea's side of the call, a blubbering mass of tears, apologizing over and over to her mom. The storm calmed and she came into the kitchen and handed the phone back to me.

"I'm booking flights home for both of them," Mrs. Brown told me. "I'll text you with the info, if you don't mind getting them to the airport there?"

"Absolutely."

The call to Rory's home didn't go quite so smoothly. At one point he stomped into the guest room and we could hear his raised voice behind the closed door.

"They never did mesh, Rory and his dad," Chelsea told me under her breath. "But hopefully my mom can help them work things out, if they can't do it on their own. She's a clinical psychologist."

I didn't comment on that, seeing as how that mother-daughter duo hadn't exactly been on the same page for a long time either. I realized I'd been up since five-ish and had not once thought of breakfast, so I went to the fridge to rummage through our provisions.

Eggs, tomatoes, a small hunk of cheese, and a packet of bacon bits—I figured I could do something with that. If I couldn't manage to correctly flip an omelet in a pan, I could certainly scramble it all together. And we had enough bread to fill out the meal with toast.

I was just breaking eggs into a bowl when Rory returned, his face flushed and his movements agitated. He set my phone on the countertop.

"Everything okay? No, wait. You don't have to answer that."

Chelsea stepped over to set a hand on his shoulder.

"Look, you guys are welcome to hang out in the back yard, sit under the gazebo or something, if you'd like. Breakfast will be ready in less than ten minutes."

The sight of pending food seemed to appeal to both of them, and they took my suggestion willingly enough. I was buttering the bread slices for the air fryer when my phone pinged with an incoming text, the flight schedule from Chelsea's mother.

I opened the message with my only non-greasy finger and read it. They were on a Southwest Airlines flight leaving here at two p.m. I breathed a sigh of relief. A couple hours from now I could see them safely into the custody of the airport system, my duty done, and from there it was out of my hands.

Conversation remained minimal as we ate. Both of my guests had plenty on their minds, and I let them mull over their own thoughts. Rory offered to do the dishes, and Chelsea went into their room to separate the borrowed clothing from their own, starting a load of laundry even though I assured her I could do that later. Eventually, I parked them in front of the TV while I sent Drake another text, praying to hear something soon. Meanwhile, I caught up on emails and other work stuff, until it was time to leave for the airport.

The departure area lanes were jammed with cars and people.

"You can just let us out here," Rory said, reaching for the door handle.

But I still felt the weight of responsibility. Plus, he seemed to forget they had no tickets and no phones with all the data for the flight. "I know. But I'd feel better if I made sure everything was in order before driving away. It'll only take a few extra minutes to park."

I wheeled around to the garage entrance, and had to drive to the third level before an empty space showed up. Rory was giving me an I-told-you-so look, but I managed to ignore it. Inside, at the check-in kiosk, I used the ticketing info Mrs. Brown had sent to my phone and the machine spat out old-fashioned paper boarding passes for them.

"Okay, we want to head for the escalators," I told them. "Security is on the second level."

Again, he sent the we're-not-children attitude, and again I ignored it. I can be an impossibly old thirty-something at times.

As we pushed our way through the throngs, Chelsea froze, her eyes wide.

"What? Keep moving, hon." I reached out to touch her shoulder.

Her eyes were on the line of people winding their way to the Southwest Airlines ticket counter. "Georgie," she breathed.

There he was. He must have been getting himself a ticket back to Texas. Could we have had any more rotten stroke of bad luck? And now he'd spotted us. He ducked to pass under the strap that formed the ticketing queue.

Chelsea started toward the exit doors to the street, but I yanked her back. Pointing to our right, I gave her a shove and grabbed Rory's arm at the same time. "Escalators— run!"

They followed instructions without hesitation and I plowed in right after them. We dodged people who gave us annoyed glances as we cut through and started taking the escalator stairs two at a time. At the top I took a quick peek back.

Georgie was already halfway up, and he wasn't even being polite as he shoved other people aside.

"Keep going!" I caught up with Chelsea and directed her toward the security lanes.

Georgie was less than forty feet behind us. "Stop that woman," he yelled. "She's kidnapping my kids!"

Good one. A few people actually gave us an extra glance, trying to assess the situation.

"Not true!" I shouted back. "He's a criminal and he's after all of us!"

A burly man stepped forward, taking in a scruffy, unshaven man with stringy hair and filthy jeans chasing a fairly average woman with two young people who, thankfully, were now wearing clean clothes and had that freshly-showered look about them. The man tried to block Georgie's way, but the weasel ducked around him. He was less than twenty feet away now.

The line for security wound around in a snaking procession, and my heart thudded to a stop. I'd never get the kids in there quickly enough.

At the entrance, two TSA officers were in the process of checking boarding passes and IDs.

"Have your wallets ready and go for the shorter line," I urged, giving Chelsea a tiny push in that direction. Rory followed.

I spun toward Georgie, fixing my stance wide and my gaze on those cold, blue eyes of his. The burly man, another passenger, had caught up with us. "Need some help?"

He didn't wait for an answer, but called out to a uniformed officer who started to hurry toward us.

"What's the problem here?" the officer asked. His uniform told me he was APD.

But Georgie was done. He spun around like a mini tornado on a path, and raced back through the wide corridor, toward the exits.

"Catch him! He's a killer, wanted in New Mexico and Texas."

The cop keyed a small microphone on his shoulder and murmured some sort of code words. Frankly, my heart was racing too hard to concentrate on much of anything except the fact that Georgie was now out of sight, somewhere down the escalator.

"I've got officers waiting at the exit doors," he said. "Now, you want to tell me what this is about?"

I craned my neck around him, making sure Chelsea and Rory were safely under the watchful eyes of airport security. Then I outlined everything for the cop, showing my ID, and ending by giving him the names of contacts within the Albuquerque police, state police, and DEA who'd been working hard to catch Georgie Lafarge.

"He killed a man in Texas, an aircraft mechanic named Benjamin Estevez. He's been chasing this young couple for a week or more. They've already given their statements to the authorities."

The police officer, who gave the impression his most complicated duties involved giving breathalyzer tests on Saturday nights, gave a slow nod. "All righty then."

I stuck close by until my young friends were approaching the scanning portion of the routine. I caught sight of Chelsea, who gave me a timid wave before walking on toward the airline gates.

Chapter 25

Two hours later, Sally handed me a mug with some kind of herbal tea, and Ron seemed a little incredulous as I talked. "And so I walked out of the airport in the company of this cop who wasn't sure whether to believe my story or not ... But when we got to the curb and he saw two other officers shoving Georgie into the back of a cruiser, I felt a bit vindicated."

We were in Ron's office upstairs. He reached for his phone and placed a call to someone at APD, one of his many contacts who knew him well enough to share information.

"It all checks out," he said. "Lafarge is downtown in a cell. It's still early in the process, but it looks like he'll be extradited to Texas. The various agencies have to get their

Deceptions Can Be Murder

stories put together as to whether they can keep him here on kidnapping and grand theft charges, or if the murder in Dallas trumps that. Chances are, he'll stand trial in both states, eventually."

I relaxed back in the chair for the first time since … well, since I could remember. There hadn't been one relaxing moment since John Flick walked in here to hire us.

"Flick. What's going to happen to him?"

Ron gave a shrug. "Again, that's for the higher-ups. I'm thinking DEA will swoop in and gather all the evidence they can, trying to get some drug trafficking charges that will stick."

"Wow. I wonder how Drake will take that news."

"Probably like anyone who's had a friend that went off the rails. Sorry it happened, but realizing the friend made his own choices along the way."

I sipped my tea and digested that information for a few minutes. I hadn't especially admired John Flick, but something still didn't sit right about the drug charges. Somehow, I didn't pick up those kind of vibes from him.

My phone went off with a text. Good news. Chelsea and Rory were back in San Diego safely. Her parents had just picked them up at the airport there. For me, it was mission accomplished. For them, I suspected they still had some issues to resolve and a lot of work ahead.

I debated whether to go home and take a much-needed day to do nothing but veg in front of the TV with a whole season of *The Big Bang Theory*, or to check my office computer and lose myself in routine matters such as journal entries and billing statements. I'd missed the deadline to mail our estimated tax payments for the quarter, so there was always that little task to get out of the way. Somewhere in the midst of procrastinating on all this,

Sally buzzed to let us know John Flick was on the phone.

Ron raised an eyebrow as he picked up the call. He put it on speaker.

"Ron, Charlie! I need help—this can't be happening." His words came in urgent whispers.

"Hello, John. I'm afraid I don't know what you mean," Ron responded. "What, exactly, is happening?"

I sent my brother a devilish little smile.

"They're raiding my offices. Harrison has been taken away in handcuffs. What the hell!"

Ron played it, drawing out the agony. "Who's raiding the offices, John? I didn't know anyone was coming there."

Technically true, although we'd been given a pretty clear hint of it.

"The DEA, you nitwit!"

"What are they accusing you of?"

Paper rustled in the background. "I don't know—I never read this stuff! They come marching in here with this warrant or whatever it is, and then they're pulling out file drawers and filling cardboard boxes—with my stuff!"

I *almost* felt the teeniest bit sorry for him. I could envision the helpless feeling of having your offices torn apart by officials who wouldn't tell you anything in the process.

"This is all your fault, Charlie Parker! You'll be hearing from my lawyers!"

Now that could get interesting.

A no-nonsense female voice interrupted in the background. "Mr. Flick, you'll need to come with us."

"John, I'd suggest you use your one phone call to reach out to those lawyers, rather than chewing me out."

There were shuffling movements in the distance, his

voice saying "wait a minute" and the call abruptly ended.

Ron and I exchanged a look. "Could this actually bounce back on us in some way?" I asked.

"I don't see how. We were hired to find a van. We did. Everything else ties back to Flick's operation."

But I still had a whole lot of questions. Could it be that Harrison Stoker was the insider at Flick Helicopters who was in deep with the Mexican cartels, or were John and Harrison in this together? And what about Georgie Lafarge—was he in on the drug dealings, just a petty auto thief, or merely a cold-blooded killer?

Chapter 26

Ron suggested I go home and get some sleep. Yeah, right. As if. My stomach was still a little queasy at the thought of how close I'd come to being sliced open by Lafarge.

But I did need to check in on Elsa. I'd definitely fallen down in those duties these past couple of days. I phoned her and told her I would bring dinner. She requested Pedro's green chile chicken enchiladas, which was an easy yes for me. I envisioned an evening with a filling dinner, followed by some TV time, during which I would probably doze off. Gram's favorites were ancient reruns of Lawrence Welk and his champagne music style. As I said, easy for me to fall asleep to. Which I did.

Of course, the downside to falling asleep in the early

evening is that I found myself wide awake from about midnight onward. A fierce thunderstorm woke me with a sharp crack of thunder and lightning. I went to the bedroom window, which was streaming with rain. It continued to pound on the roof for more than a half hour, and I really hoped the parts of Arizona with the fires were getting at least this much. I wanted my sweetheart home.

At that point, falling back asleep was nothing more than a wish. My nerve endings tingled and my eyelids refused to close. I pulled on lightweight sweats and padded through to the kitchen. While the kettle heated for tea, I burned off some excess energy by wiping down the cabinets and cleaning the microwave. And although I'd envisioned burrowing into the corner of the sofa quietly, I caught myself pacing the living room. I repeatedly looked at my phone screen, on the off chance that Drake had responded to my messages and they'd somehow fallen into a time delay. Or maybe he was as sleepless as I, and we could actually talk.

But no. The silence was beginning to worry me, even as I chided myself for expecting to hear anything in the middle of the night.

I logged onto my favorite weather tracking site and watched in real time as the big storm continued to move over Albuquerque. Sadly, it showed that none of this weather was passing through Arizona. It had approached us from the north, the way winter storms normally do. I wondered if I could enact some type of mind-over-matter power and get it to shove westward by five hundred miles. And then I realized how stupid it sounded, just having that thought.

I switched my herbal tea for a glass of wine.

The intensity of the storm seemed to be lessening, and

I shifted away from the weather site to another one with regional news stories. Spent a half hour sipping my wine and scrolling mindlessly. Until the name Trinidad popped out at me.

Police officials and fire department volunteers from Trinidad and nearby Raton were called out to respond to a cabin fire near the small community of Starkville in the early evening hours of June 18th after a neighboring property owner phoned in the alarm. In this heavily wooded area, with dry conditions all month, the fire was treated as an 'extreme emergency' and responders immediately converged on the site. The neighbor reported that "A guy in a blue truck, driving like a madman, passed me on the road less than an hour before I smelled the smoke. I called it in right away."

Luckily, the fire teams were able to contain the blaze to the lone cabin. No other structures were harmed and the surrounding forest land was spared.

Two days ago. The timing seemed to fit with that evening when Lafarge had left Chelsea and Rory tied up in the barn while he went to look for the cash. When he didn't find it, my guess was he struck out in anger to burn down the whole place. When he'd arrived back at the barn afterward, he most certainly was in a murderous rage. Thank God we three had been able to escape him.

But was there some way Georgie Lafarge knew who I was? Could he be cooling his heels and plotting revenge for my part in foiling his big plans?

Charlie, stop it! He's locked up. If they haven't already taken him back to Texas, that's happening soon.

I switched off my computer, rinsed the wine glass, and tried to think of any tried-and-true ways to fall asleep. Hot chocolate; I'd already consumed two beverages so that was an invitation to multiple bathroom trips. A boring book; nothing on the shelves caught my attention. More Lawrence Welk; sorry, wouldn't be able to take that. I finally plopped down on the sofa and pulled a throw over my legs. Freckles had long since decided my rambling and agitated state wasn't for her—she moved over to let me lie down, then snuggled against my feet. I tried some deep breathing exercises, fell into a pattern of mimicking the dog's even pattern, and that's how I fell asleep.

It was after nine when the ping of an incoming text grabbed my attention. I groaned and sat up, remembering now that our sofa is not exactly back-friendly as an all-night place to sleep. When the second ping happened, I tracked my phone to the dining table, where I'd been seated with my laptop last night.

Rubbing grainy sleep stuff from my eyes, I tapped the phone and saw, to my disappointment, that the message wasn't from Drake. The electric company was letting me know they'd processed my automatic credit card payment. Ugh. I woke up for this?

I set up the coffee maker, yawned and stretched, and looked out the back window toward Gram's. There she was, wearing her big sun hat and plucking an apricot from the tree. I stepped out to my back porch.

"Hey, I'll come over in a while and help you pick those," I called out.

"I think there's enough ripe ones to make a little batch of jam." She looked more closely at me and chuckled. "Your hair looks like you slept in it, kiddo."

It was one of her famous teasing comments from when I was little. And I supposed she was right. I reached up to rake my fingers through the strands and discovered more than a few tangles.

"Take your time, hon. I'll take these in the house, but I'll save the real work for when you're here."

"Give me time to check in and clean up. Maybe thirty minutes, an hour?"

I phoned the office while I put away a big mug of coffee and a slice of toast. Sally assured me all was well. Ron had gone to a meeting with the big client for whom he'd been working on employee background checks all month long. No one, it seemed, wanted me for anything. If I was supposed to be sad about that, well, I wasn't.

Drake was my bigger worry. I'd sent three texts over the course of twenty-four hours, a couple more yesterday. And while I was trying to keep my tone upbeat and breezy, I had to admit I was becoming increasingly concerned. There were other channels I could check, but contacting the FAA would unleash all sorts of official missing-aircraft procedures. That was something I would resort to only if I absolutely knew he was missing.

The Forest Service was officially his employer on this job, but that, too, was a tangle of officialdom. We'd been through this once, me trying to reach Drake while out on a job, and my inquiry was met with something along the lines, of "what's wrong little lady, hubby not on a short enough leash" and Drake receiving some humiliating teasing at his end of the line.

No, I was not going to do anything official. No doubt he'd checked in at the firebase when he returned to Heber after his service inspection was finished. If he hadn't, they would have been calling me. They would have also contacted me if something—heaven forbid—happened during one of his flights.

I paced the length of the house one extra time and

told myself to drop it. My husband was an excellent pilot (that safety award!). I'd just been through a worrisome experience of my own, and I wanted the reassurance that my little family was all right. Just because Drake was busy with more important things, or his phone was out of signal range, or something ... I needed to grow up. And I really needed to deal with what was real, not imagine myself into what Gram would surely call a tizzy.

And on that note, I walked over next door to spend the rest of the morning making apricot jam.

Chapter 27

The unresolved threads began coming together shortly after we'd finished making the jam and I looked out Elsa's front window to see Dottie's car pulling into the driveway. I stepped out to the porch to help carry her bags, but she didn't have much.

"Just this one," she said, huffing a little as she lifted a large roller bag that must have surely incurred an extra charge at the airline.

I took the handle and wheeled it to the front door, asking how her daughter's family were doing.

"Oh, I think they're all fixed up. For now, anyhow." She gave a tired smile, which brightened considerably when she saw Elsa in the doorway.

"You're just in time for biscuits and jam," Gram told

her. "That is, if you want to make some of your fabulous biscuits ..."

Dottie laughed and readily agreed. While the two of them puttered in the kitchen, I excused myself to run home. I'd only then realized I'd left my phone there. After all my earlier worries, apparently when I told myself to drop it, I really had managed to do so.

Two texts and one missed call awaited me.

The call: "Hi, hon, so sorry I've been out of cell range so long. Things are okay. Talk soon."

First text: **Meant to say rain's predicted. Pray hard.**

Second text (from Linda): **Hey, so sorry I rushed out the other day. A makeup lunch? Call me.**

I responded to Drake's text by promising to send some of our rain in his direction. Texted Linda to set up something for later in the day, suggesting she phone me when she was at a stopping point. We ended up planning to meet for a drink instead, at a favorite place that was halfway between her office and mine.

After checking next door to be sure the ladies were getting settled back into their routine, I showered and changed into fresh jeans and a pretty, shimmery top. I had two hours before I would meet up with Linda, and since I hadn't appeared at the office all day, maybe it was time.

Ever since my obvious distress this morning, Freckles would not leave my side. I finally gave in and let her come along. I would put her in her crate at the office while I ducked out to see Linda, then I'd pick up my pup on the way home.

Ron had returned from his big meeting, happy to say that the client was more than satisfied with our work. He handed me a check with a very decent number of digits before the comma.

"Nice."

"And they want me to continue doing the same backgrounds for their other offices on both coasts."

"Excellent. Glad our detour to handle the Flick case didn't mess up anything with Borkin." I promptly logged the payment on their account and then snapped a photo and made the online deposit.

Ron looked like he was preparing to leave for the day, but I spent a few minutes filling him in on other current events—Dottie's arrival at Gram's, the plea from Arizona for some rain. As if to punctuate that statement, a dark cloud moved across the sun and dimmed the light in my office. I also told him about the story I'd found, about the cabin fire in Colorado and how I felt fairly sure it was the same place Chelsea and Rory had hidden out for several days.

"Have they actually moved Georgie Lafarge back to Texas?" I tried to sound casual about it, not admitting how much of my sleepless night had dwelled upon this. We'd closed our case. We were done.

He shrugged. "Want me to track down somebody at APD and ask?"

"We can check on it tomorrow. You're ready to go home and I'm heading out for a drink with an old friend."

I bribed the dog with a cookie and she trotted happily to the door of her crate. Leaving a couple lights on, I walked downstairs with Ron and we parted, just as a few fat raindrops hit the cars.

It was less than a ten minute drive to the La Posada Hotel, with its classy bar that catered to the business crowd, and where women could meet for chats without the hassle of being hit on. The rain never really developed along my route, but that's the nature of storms around here. One place can be pounded, while a block away the streets are dry.

Linda's Tesla pulled in, only moments behind me. We walked in and found a booth in a quiet corner.

"How's your dad?" I immediately asked.

She drooped a little. "Hanging in there. He's in and out, not really sure where he is. It's sad."

Our server brought a basket of chips and took our drink orders. I picked up a chip, dunked it in the salsa, and looked up to see Linda watching me.

"How are you, I have to ask. What's with the dark circles under your eyes?"

And here I thought I'd covered those up. "Not sleeping very well. Usually when Drake's away I adapt pretty well, but ... I don't know. Probably it's because of this case we just wrapped up."

"I can prescribe you something, if you want."

I waved off the suggestion. "Eventually I'll just get tired enough and then I'll get a good, full night's sleep." When she didn't appear appeased, I promised I'd call her if this kept up more than another week.

Our glasses of wine arrived, and the subject turned to an idea we'd played around with, six or eight months ago, the thought that we girls should take a trip together somewhere. Before either of us knew it, an hour had slipped by, then nearly two hours.

"I gotta go," she said. "I don't want to miss the evening visiting hours at Dad's place."

"And I've got a doggie who'll be supremely upset that she hasn't got her dinner yet."

We split the check and headed out, hugging as we each got into our vehicles. When I got to the office, I opted to park at the curb out front, rather than driving to the back parking spaces. I'd unlocked the front door and walked in before I realized something was off.

We always left a lamp on Sally's credenza turned on at night. It was. I'd also left the light on in my office, as company for Freckles. But the stairway sconces were on now. I was certain I had flicked that switch off. Then I spotted wet footprints coming from the kitchen. The hairs on my arms prickled.

I almost called out to Ron, but something held me back. The wet prints were too fresh. Then I heard Freckles whimper. A heavy footfall sounded above my head. The dog's metal crate rattled, as if kicked, and my baby started to bark ferociously.

I reached for my bag and realized I'd left it in the Jeep. My phone was in it. My pistol was in the glovebox. Shit. We had an intruder who was about to hurt my dog and I couldn't do anything about it. I scanned the reception area for ideas, my eyes lighting on the landline on Sally's desk. I scooped up the receiver and dialed 911. The operator quickly answered and asked the nature of my emergency.

Under my breath, I muttered a quick explanation that I thought there was an intruder in my office. As the dispatcher was telling me she would send the police, a footstep sounded, a loud creak on the third step from the bottom.

"Thanks, Mom, that would be great."

"Is the intruder in the room with you?"

"That's exactly right, Mom."

"Police are on the w—" And the rest of her words were lost when a hand snatched the receiver from me and slammed it down.

Chapter 28

I looked up into the cold, blue eyes of Georgie Lafarge. His stringy brown hair was matted against his head, his clothing wet and shoes muddy. He wore an orange jailhouse jumpsuit with a dark windbreaker over it. In his right hand was the letter opener from my desk, a pointy, deadly looking thing.

Stall, Charlie. All I could hope was that the police really were on the way.

The phone began to ring, a sharp trill that always seemed normal during business hours and now shrieked in my ears. I glanced at it. Line four. It had to be Ron. Back in the days before we all carried cell phones all the time, we'd established the code as a way for us to reach each other outside business hours, when we didn't want to pick up line one. I automatically reached for it.

Georgie had other ideas. The sharp tip of the letter opener touched my throat.

I pulled my hand away from the phone and held both hands out to the sides, open and visible. "Okay, right. I won't answer." I took a tiny step back. His breath reeked of onions.

"How did you know to find me here?" Stalling, stalling.

"Oh, I knew that, even before the airport," he gloated. "Figured out whose stolen van I had, and it was simple enough to learn that an Albuquerque investigator had been hired to get it back. When the little bimbo redhead shouted 'Charlie' it didn't take a lot to put it together."

"Pretty smart."

"I can so add up two and two." His eyes had taken on a faraway look.

I had no idea what that meant, but I didn't trust he was so far away that he wouldn't make a grab for me if I ran. *Keep stalling.*

"So, what do you want from us?"

He came back to the present. "The cash, of course."

"Cash?" I didn't actually, for one minute, think he would buy any claim that I had no idea there was cash involved.

He didn't. His eyes glittered dangerously and he closed the gap between us, grabbing my arm and twisting it behind me. The letter opener poked the side of my neck again. I was listening like crazy for the blessed sound of sirens and heard nothing. Nothing but a whimper from upstairs.

I spun away from Georgie, wrenching my shoulder in the process. "Did you hurt my dog, you monster?"

He grinned, and I saw the insanity behind those cold

eyes. Maybe if I could keep him talking …

I tried again. "Okay, I know there was some cash, but trust me, I don't have it."

"Then we'll take a little ride and you'll get it for me."

"Mr. Lafarge—"

"*Mister* is my father, and don't you ever bring up that bastard to me." He gave my arm another yank.

"Sorry. Sorry! Georgie … let's think this through. I'm pretty sure I can't get my hands on the cash."

He held up the check from our client, which he must have picked up from my desk and stuffed into a pocket. "We'll just wait here until the bank opens in the morning and you'll walk up and cash this for me then."

Um … I'd already deposited it to the business and made note of that, so clearly, he didn't know how these things are done. I needed to work that to my advantage. I pretended to give his idea serious consideration.

"Right. Well, then we have to wait here until morning. If you don't hurt me or my dog, I'll do what you said, cash the check for you." I winced a little dramatically. "And now that we have a plan, can you please let go of my wrist?"

Through the front windows I saw three cars roll to a stop across the street, lights off.

Chapter 29

I edged sideways until Georgie had to turn his back to the windows to keep an eye on me. I couldn't see what was going on in the dark, beyond some vague shadows moving about. All I could do was try to keep this madman's attention on me, so the police could get the jump on him.

"Georgie, are you hungry? There's probably some food—"

"Shut up!"

"Listen, you! You got your way. I'm handing over tens of thousands in the morning. We'll go to the bank. Can you at least be civil tonight if we're stuck here for the next nine hours?"

"Fine. Food would be okay. Whatcha got?"

I found myself actually considering the question. Sally

had stocked up on a bunch of snacks when Chelsea and Rory were here. But the faint sound of the lock turning at the kitchen door, grabbed my attention.

Georgie sensed the shift in my attention. He threw the letter opener down on Sally's desk and fumbled in the pockets of his clothing, coming out with a pistol. It looked like a standard-issue police weapon, and suddenly several things became clear.

"Georgie ... you don't want to—"

The front door slammed back against the wall at the same minute heavy footsteps pounded down the short hallway from the kitchen. Four officers drew down on the prisoner, and I dropped to the floor and rolled away behind the safety of the desk.

Shouts ordered Georgie to put down his weapon and I guess he did. The next sounds were of handcuffs clicking in place and a new set of footsteps coming from the kitchen. I opened my clenched eyes for a peek at ... *Ron?* I'd know those boots anywhere.

While they hauled Georgie (muttering something about two plus two) out to one of the cruisers, Ron shoved his pistol into its holster and reached out a hand to me.

"You okay, sis?"

I nodded. "Just feeling a little dumb because I didn't bring my weapon in with me."

He pulled me into a hug. "You didn't have any reason to. The main thing is, you're all right."

"Oh, gosh, what about Freckles? Georgie was upstairs when I got here." I don't actually recall my feet hitting the stair treads before I was up there and running into my office.

My baby was in her crate, door closed. She whimpered and wiggled all over when she saw me. "Oh, sweetie, thank goodness you're safe."

Thank goodness he hadn't let her out. This little pup would give her life for me, with no concept of how unevenly matched she might be when it came to attacking a nutcase guy like Georgie Lafarge. I hugged her squirming body, wetting the top of her head with tears, until I finally figured out all she wanted was a cookie from the tin on my bookshelf. I gave her three.

After locking up the office and promising the police I would come downtown tomorrow and sign a statement about tonight's incident, Ron followed me home. It was a nice gesture, since Drake was still away and I had to admit having a large man with a pistol nearby was something of a comfort.

He came inside with me and checked the entire house, even though logic told both of us that the killer was not there. I offered my brother food and a beer, which he accepted. While we warmed up the leftover pizza slices, I asked him to fill in the gaps.

"How did you know I was at the office and in trouble?"

He ticked the points off with his fingers. "You'd told me you were going back to get Freckles after your drink with Linda. I called your cell several times to warn you, no answer. I called the office on line four, no answer. Your being in trouble, that was just an educated guess."

"Wait—what? Warn me?"

"That Georgie Lafarge was on the loose somewhere here in the city."

I felt my eyes go wide. "How …?"

"During the extradition process. They had him out of his cell, under guard by two officers, and he managed to get hold of one of their weapons. He killed one officer and took off into the late afternoon. The story, and his picture, was on the six o'clock news."

Why had I, not once, looked for a TV set in the bar while I was out with Linda? Because it was a classy place, not a sports bar.

"I made the calls, got a bad feeling, then heard our office address on the police scanner." He gave a wide shrug. "You know the rest of it."

Chapter 30

I fell asleep soon after Ron left, but jolted awake after a couple hours, a flash of lightning and immediate crash of thunder the culprits. And no matter how diligently I tried to get back to sleep, my thoughts raced with images of crazy George and how badly this whole night could have gone. I punched my pillow, but that didn't do a lot to make me feel better.

Finally, around five a.m. I gave up the effort. Pulling my hair into a high ponytail, I grabbed a lightweight cotton robe and went to the kitchen. Freckles didn't care that it was barely gray dawn outside—she decided it was time for breakfast.

I walked out to the back porch with her, enjoying the cool dampness on my bare feet. The overnight rain had freshened everything and the storm had moved through. Thin clouds glowed with the promise of a pink sunrise and a clear day. Next door, Gram's house was dark but then the kitchen light came on. I gave a sigh, happy to know Dottie was back there.

Nearly everything felt right with the world. Our case had wrapped up, and it wasn't up to me to put away the law breakers. Other agencies, way bigger than ours, had that responsibility. I hadn't heard from Chelsea or Rory—didn't really expect to—so I had to assume they were getting their lives back together, in whatever way would work for them.

Freckles interrupted my reverie by racing past me to the door and scratching to get in. Breakfast waits for no one. I followed her inside and scooped kibble for her, then set the coffee maker to brew. My own breakfast choices were somewhat more limited. I couldn't remember the last time I'd made a grocery trip. There was some rather dry bread for toast, although I did have a jar of freshly made apricot jam to help it out.

Last night, Ron had made a point of telling me to take the day off and do nothing at all. I guess he'd seen my frazzled state after confronting the insane killer in the office (Ron can sometimes be clueless about other people's emotions). And I did still have all those episodes of *The Big Bang Theory* that could lighten the mood. Still, I felt restless. I'm not good at having nothing to do.

In lieu of standing at the kitchen window all morning and staring out into the yard, I forced myself to toast some bread, check emails while I munched it down at the kitchen table, and then head for the shower. After I finished all that, dried my hair, and dressed in some stay-home cotton shorts and shirt, I returned to the kitchen to set my plate in the dishwasher.

And that's when I saw a text from Drake: **Rain came! Meet me at Double Eagle at noon and I'll take you to Pedro's for lunch.**

Well, you don't have to issue a lunch invitation to this girl twice. It was only ten o'clock, but I zipped to the bedroom to choose something appropriate to wear for a reunion lunch with my hubby.

"Drake's coming home!" I called out to Freckles, forgetting that dogs take everything as an in-the-moment truth.

She raced to the front door and sat, eyes intent on the doorknob.

"Oh, baby, not just yet." I gave her a hug and a treat, but she didn't forget the promise.

It would take about twenty minutes to drive out to the small regional airport, and I still arrived a full half-hour early. When his aircraft came into sight and then hovered above the tarmac my heart swelled. Having our little family back together, realizing how many dangers we both had faced in recent days, I felt my eyes well up.

The moment he touched down, I let Freckles out of the Jeep and we both ran out to meet our guy. He opened his side door while going through the shut-down process, letting the dog jump onto his lap, and after the rotor blades had spun to a full stop, he got out and took me in his arms.

Smoky flight suit and all, I was never so glad to see him back home.

Epilogue

We felt the first crisp days of autumn in early September. It was during a jaunt Drake, Freckles, and I made up north for a chance to stay at a favorite place, El Monte Sagrado, and an even better chance to visit Sweet's Sweets, my favorite baker and bakery of all times.

After gorging ourselves on Samantha's amazing amaretto cheesecake, we took a stroll around the Taos Plaza, and that's when Ron's message came through: You'll want to watch the news tonight.

To be clear, I rarely *want* to watch the news, and my brother knows this. So, it had to be something personal. I showed the message to Drake, and we agreed that we could catch the early broadcast in our room and then treat ourselves to a nice dinner afterward. So, there we were at five p.m.

The lead story was about how many murders had happened in the city overnight (and this is why the news shows lost me a long time ago), but the third story in the lineup began with the teaser that there was a New Mexico connection—stay tuned.

Six men in suits stood on courthouse steps somewhere, facing a mob of reporters with microphones jammed at them like an aggressive bouquet of flowers. I recognized one of the faces. John Flick. One of the other men was talking to the reporters.

"Our client is completely innocent of all these ridiculous charges, and we are most certainly appealing today's verdict. Mr. Flick had no knowledge of any drug movement using his company equipment, and most certainly has no connection with any Mexican cartel." While the lawyer spoke, John nodded vehemently beside him.

"But evidence was found, both inside one of your company vehicles and in more than one of your helicopters," asserted one reporter. "What do you say to that?"

"Our own investigation is ongoing, but if company property was used in this manner, it was done by other employees, not Mr. Flick."

I sent Drake a skeptical look, which he matched.

The anchorperson: "That was yesterday's story, and now for further developments we go live to the Harris County District Court in Houston."

I also knew one of the faces in this crowd. Harrison Stoker, whose lawyer said very much the same thing Flick's had said, pinning the blame on the company owner, rather than the employee. Once we'd got the gist of it, I phoned

Ron and put the call on speaker for Drake's benefit.

"Aside from both these guys swearing they're complete angels and it's all the other guy's fault, what's really going to happen here?" I asked.

"The whole 'I'm so innocent, and we're appealing this all the way to the top' is just standard lawyer-speak. Both men are guilty as sin. I got hold of the court transcripts and copies of the evidence. Stoker will go to prison on drug charges, even if he does flip and give evidence against the Mexican cartel leaders. Flick will lose his business and everything he built."

Drake looked sober at the news, but unsurprised.

Ron continued. "Georgie Lafarge's trial just finished in Dallas, for murdering Benjamin Estevez. That trial won't likely make the Albuquerque news, unless our own murder rate takes a plunge. The jury unanimously voted to convict him."

"Oh yeah, what was the New Mexico connection they referred to about Flick?"

"Hm. Maybe they cut that part. But in the court testimony, it came out about the stolen van and where it was recovered, and the fact that a local Albuquerque private investigator was instrumental in the capture of Georgie Lafarge."

I swallowed hard. "But I'm not the licensed inves—"

"Since when have you ever known the media to get all their facts right?"

True.

My phone rang with another incoming call, one I really should take, so I disconnected from Ron.

"Hello, Chelsea. How are you?"

"Charlie! Charlie! Have you seen the news?"

I laughed. "Yes, and it sounds good, doesn't it?"

"Rory and I testified. It was scary, seeing that awful Georgie in the courtroom. But we told the judge what happened. I told them how you saved us, when he came back to the barn. He would have killed us." Her voice broke a little, and that made my throat tighten with emotion.

These poor kids went through so much. My scary encounter in the office that night was … well, yeah, it was awful in that moment. But when I thought about what this young couple endured and how frightened they must have been … I took a deep breath before I could speak again.

"And things at home? Is it better?"

There was a long moment of silence. "Yeah. We're getting there." She sniffed. "Charlie, I want to thank you, for everything. I never had the courage to really voice my needs, and my parents never listened. It took this … this *thing*, and then you speaking with them on my behalf. We have a ways to go, but the communication is so much better."

"And Rory? He's doing okay?"

"He's doing okay. I don't know if there's a future for us. But I do believe we'll both come out stronger on the other side of this."

"Chelsea—I'm glad. You take care of yourself."

She must have been nodding but all I heard were sniffles and a faint, "I will."

At the beginning of the summer, did I have any clue about how this case would end? No. But her call made it all worth doing. And then I caught myself sniffling a little bit too. Freckles noticed and came over to lick a tear or two off my chin.

Author's Note

My regular readers already know that the seeds of ideas for many of my stories are based on some little thing in real life. In this case, I witnessed something that piqued my interest. For several weeks I'd noticed a young couple driving a beat-up van around town. Then one day it ended up parked in an empty field across from my house. And it stayed there for more than two weeks. What was this young couple's story? What was in the van? My writerly brain could not let it go.

As I began toying with ideas for some type of backstory to form the basis of this novel, I decided the opening needed to be an older woman's observations about what was going on in her neighborhood. We all know the nosy neighbor … well, in this case that nosy one was me.

In real life, the van just went away at some point, and I never did learn who they were or what was in there (if anything at all). But since when do those little details stop a fiction writer, especially one who just has to make a mystery out of everything? I hope you enjoyed this one!

Now for the important stuff. I want to give my very heartfelt thanks to my wonderful editor, Stephanie Dewey, and her fabulous team of beta readers, without whom this book would have gotten through with at least a dozen typos. To Sandra Anderson, Susan Gross, Dawn Hasiotis, Marcia Koopmann, Eve Osborne, Isobel Tamney, and Paula Webb … thank you, so very much! And to you, my readers. You are the magical ingredient that makes this writing journey so worthwhile for me.

Thank you for taking the time to read *Deceptions Can Be Murder*. If you enjoyed it, please consider telling your friends or posting a short review. Word of mouth is an author's best friend and is much appreciated.

Thank you,

Connie

* * *

There's more coming for Charlie and family!
In the meantime, if you've missed any…
Turn the page to get the links to all my books.

Next up, a new Samantha Sweet!

* * *

Sign up for Connie Shelton's free mystery newsletter at www.connieshelton.com and receive advance information about new books, along with a chance at prizes, discounts and other mystery news!

Contact by email: connie@connieshelton.com
Follow Connie Shelton on Twitter, Pinterest and Facebook

Books by Connie Shelton

The Charlie Parker Series
Deadly Gamble
Vacations Can Be Murder
Partnerships Can Be Murder
Small Towns Can Be Murder
Memories Can Be Murder
Honeymoons Can Be Murder
Reunions Can Be Murder
Competition Can Be Murder
Balloons Can Be Murder
Obsessions Can Be Murder
Gossip Can Be Murder
Stardom Can Be Murder
Phantoms Can Be Murder
Buried Secrets Can Be Murder
Legends Can Be Murder
Weddings Can Be Murder
Alibis Can Be Murder
Escapes Can Be Murder
Old Bones Can Be Murder
Sweethearts Can Be Murder
Money Can Be Murder
Road Trips Can Be Murder
Cruises Can Be Murder
Deceptions Can Be Murder
Holidays Can Be Murder - a Christmas novella

Children's Books
Daisy and Maisie and the Great Lizard Hunt
Daisy and Maisie and the Lost Kitten

The Samantha Sweet Series

Sweet Masterpiece
Sweet's Sweets
Sweet Holidays
Sweet Hearts
Bitter Sweet
Sweets Galore
Sweets Begorra
Sweet Payback
Sweet Somethings
Sweets Forgotten
Spooky Sweet
Sticky Sweet
Sweet Magic
Deadly Sweet Dreams
The Ghost of Christmas Sweet
Tricky Sweet
Haunted Sweets
Secret Sweets
Spellbound Sweets – a Halloween novella
Thankful Sweets – a Thanksgiving novella
The Woodcarver's Secret – the series prequel

The Heist Ladies Series

Diamonds Aren't Forever
The Trophy Wife Exchange
Movie Mogul Mama
Homeless in Heaven
Show Me the Money